THE BIG CASINO:
Incident in Avalon

Gig Goodloe

Llumina Press

ISBN: 978-1-62550-372-5

Dedicated to my dad,
Capt. James G. Goodloe (USAAF) (USAF) Ret.

Introduction

Ocean Park was the amusement capital of the entire Southern California coastal area. The main focal area was the huge, magnificent, first-run Dome Theatre, located on the boardwalk at the junction of the pier, which extended far out over the beautiful, blue, rambunctious Pacific Ocean.

The boardwalk was neither wood nor really a walkway. It was a wide expanse of concrete that ran through Ocean Park south to the city of Venice, separating the ocean and clean, white beach from the residential area of ramshackle beach cabins, magnificent mansions, and mid-size, well-maintained homes of retirees living out their days basking in the warm sun and gentle ocean breezes.

The pier abutting the boardwalk was the heart of the fun zone. At the far end was one of its major attractions. The Cyclone roller coaster ride was a high, fast, twisting, rip-roaring, breathtaking experience. On both sides of the pier, from the boardwalk to the Cyclone, were all manner of dinero-extracting attractions, such as shooting galleries, deep-sea dives, baseball throws, cotton candy, dime tosses, hot dogs, bumper cars, a merry-go-round, the House of Mirrors, a huge Ferris wheel, loop-the-loop side shows—just about everything one could find at a large county fair, and a great deal more. It was a big, exciting, wonderful place to live, work, play, and thoroughly enjoy.

Just north of the pier, on the ocean side of the boardwalk, was a magnificent ballroom—an immense, delightful, dime-a-dance emporium with subtle lighting, tasteful appointments and a smooth-as-glass dance floor. The ballroom featured the very best of the 40s big dance bands and world-class dance contests of every variety.

The rest of the pier area on the inland side of the boardwalk was a typical beach town—restaurants, hot-dog stands, and novelty shops. Down the middle of the boardwalk, south of the main pier, was the Lick Pier Ballroom, which featured Lawrence Welk and his soon-to-be-famous bubble machine.

As was my usual routine, I walked down the boardwalk to my office, located next to the Dome Theatre, the centerpiece of this beautiful, crazy, haphazard, delightful, carefree, life-loving community. Looking forward to a busy day, I had arrived early, after stopping long enough for a cup of coffee at a nice little restaurant on the boardwalk. I strolled toward my office humming along with Jimmy Dorsey's rendition of "Tangerine" as sung by Ray Eberly and Helen O'Connel. The catchy arrangement had come to be the standard of the 40s' war years.

I spent WWII sighting through a Norden bombsight and incinerating or pulverizing every papier-mache hamlet between the Marianas and Tokyo from five to twenty-five thousand feet aboard a B-29 Superfortress.

We all put our private lives on hold during those years and were just now beginning to pick up where we left off from what seemed an entire lifetime ago. Little did I realize that a phone call was about to change my life dramatically—yet again.

My name is Dugan, Travis Dugan; I'm a PI.

Chapter 1

The Cruise

The fog was thick. Heavy mist covered the worn decks of the old tug as she slowly felt her way out of the harbor. The night was cold, dark, and eerily quiet, except for the rumble of the diesel and the consistent thump below deck of what was probably a bent prop shaft.

The foghorn at the end of the breakwater moaned its lonely call, and the tug's horn answered as she passed from the calm, silent waters of the harbor to the open sea and on across the channel to Avalon.

I wiped the moisture from the brim of my hat and pulled the collar of my coat tight. The old man opened the door from the bridge and called down, "Hey, young fella, why don't ya come up and get outta the weather?"

I climbed the ladder to the bridge and entered the wheel-house. It was dark, except for the glow from the compass mounted above the ship's wheel. The aged wooden decks and bulkheads creaked and groaned as the tug climbed and fell from one swell to another.

"Captain Wally at your service," the old man said with a wide, toothless grin. "Must be pretty importan' business to bring a polliwog like you out on a night like this. A good lookin' young scrapper like yourself is more likely to take the big white steamer on a nice, sunny afternoon."

Spoken rhetorically, he didn't really expect an answer, and I wasn't inclined to give him one. Instead, he uncorked a tarnished silver flask and took a long pull on it before passing it to me.

"Thanks, Skipper," I said as I tipped high and eagerly waited for the smooth warmth to course through me.

1

The man cackled with delight as my eyes watered, and I coughed uncontrollably, trying unsuccessfully to pass the flask back to the old rooster. He could hardly contain his laughter and persistently pushed the flask back to me. "It's much better the second time around, ya young polliwog," he chuckled.

I was no stranger to rotgut and had spent more nights than I cared, or was able, to remember in the waterfront dives along the harbor, but this was pirate rum and had no smooth edges. It burnt your gullet all the way down and back. But the old man was right; after my palate had been thoroughly scorched, the second pull had a comforting warmth, and the chill seemed to fade. I passed the flask back and gazed out into the misty darkness.

In my line of work, missing persons and divorce cases are your bread and butter. You pad your expenses and pay your rent with them. Even so, it doesn't mean I gotta like 'em. They're always petty, messy little affairs, where nobody wins except the attorneys; everybody else escapes into the bottle. But there was something intriguing about this case. That something was Mrs. Lara Rigney.

The Rigney family was an American industrial icon. Perhaps not in the same league with the Gettys, Vanderbilts, or Rockefellers as far as power and stature, but they definitely were in the same neighborhood, and their offspring cavorted in the same international playgrounds.

Mr. R.J. Rigney, my client's father-in-law, built a confection business into a worldwide empire through diversification, hostile takeovers, and the accumulation of vast amounts of real estate.

The Rigneys owned Santa Catalina Island and had established a virtual kingdom twenty-six miles off the Southern California coast—twenty-three miles outside the US territorial limit, in international waters. The Rigneys owned the island, the casino, the town, and the steamer that brought the rich and famous from around the world to the island from L.A. to gamble and party. Catalina was becoming the "Monaco of the Pacific."

R.J., the patriarch, and his playboy son Johnny controlled everything and everybody coming to and from the island. They ruled with an iron fist cloaked in velvet. Catalina was an island haven for Hollywood movie stars and movie moguls, as well as being the glamorous, off-the-beaten-path, chic stopover for internationally known, well-heeled aristocrats, royals, sheiks, and charlatans. They were the movers and shakers of the world—and with them came mystery and intrigue. By the time the faint glow of Avalon appeared through the fog, the captain and I had almost emptied the flask of pirate rum. The foghorn sounded from the entrance to Avalon harbor and we began our approach to the empty, dark pier.

She stood in a hazy glow beneath a flashing neon bait sign. The hair on the back of my neck bristled. The feeling of a fly being lured to a spider began to creep up on me—the same uneasiness I had felt when she first phoned me. But like before, there was something about this dame I couldn't resist. Her voice was a breathy mix of silk and sandpaper. I knew I shouldn't go, but I went just the same.

As the tug pulled up to the dock, I saw she was a tall, auburn-haired beauty. Even from that distance, I knew she was a class act from head to toe. She was a thoroughbred.

I jumped to the dock and waved to Captain Wally. He waved as the tug pulled away and disappeared into the dark mist. A light, steady rain began to fall as I approached where she waited.

"Hello, Mrs. Rigney," I said. "My name is Dugan, Travis Dugan."

She stood motionless, exhaled the smoke from her cigarette, and watched as it rose and disappeared into the fog. Her gorgeous brown eyes stared deep into mine then she performed a slow, lingering scan from my top to my bottom and back again. "I'm glad you could make it on such short notice," she finally said. "I'll explain tomorrow when I take you to meet my father-in-law. My car is parked in back; I'll take you to your hotel."

3

She let the cigarette fall from her fingers and crushed it out with an expensive Italian pump.

She drove up the hill and around the backside of Avalon, eventually turning back toward the harbor. She pulled to a stop at the curb in front of a clapboard rooming house. She apologized again for the accommodations and said she would return in the morning. She handed me a room key and said goodnight. I stepped into the rain and watched as she drove away into the night.

I woke to the morning sun streaming through tattered curtains that fluttered in the ocean breeze. I leaned out of the window and inhaled a big breath of sea air. It was a bright, sunny morning, and the harbor was a pale blue, filled with pricey yachts and small fishing boats.

As I gazed on the harbor, I heard a board creak on the third step as someone came up the stairs at the end of the hall. I waited, and then heard the slight creak of the floorboard two rooms down from mine. I looked under the door as a shadow stopped at my room. There was a soft knock on the door.

"Who's there?" I asked.

"It's Mrs. O'Malley. I've brought some clean towels for you, son," came a gentle Irish brogue from the other side of the door. I opened the door, and there stood a sweet, little, cherub-faced lady with fresh towels neatly folded over her arm.

"Top-a-the-marnin' to you, Mr. Dugan," she said as she waddled in with a slight limp that made her sway from side to side when she walked. "I heard you come in late last night; I thought you might could use some fresh towels. I'll be back in a bit to make up the room." She went about stripping the sheets and pillowcases from the bed. She gathered the bed linens and the used towels and headed for the door. "If you need anything washed, just leave it by the door, and I'll get to it when I bring fresh linens. You better get a move on; Mrs. Rigney will be along any time now." With that, she closed the door behind her and headed back down the hall.

I quickly washed and shaved, grabbed my hat and coat, and made my way downstairs. I got out front just as Mrs. Rigney arrived. I got in, and once again, she drove around the backside of town, high up into the hills.

In the morning light, she was even more beautiful than I had remembered. Her skin was the color of fresh, smooth peaches, and her eyes were large and almond-shaped. As we drove, the sun peeked through the trees, showing off her long auburn hair and rich, full lips.

She had gorgeous legs, delicate at the ankle. She was a stunning beauty, in her late twenties or early thirties, and I couldn't keep my eyes off her.

She turned and caught me staring. A knowing smile slowly formed, and her face brightened. "Enjoying the scenery this morning, Mr. Dugan?" she asked coyly.

"Breathtaking," was my only response.

We made our way along narrow, rain-washed streets over-hung with lush green trees. The smell of wet pavement drying in the morning sun always brought back fond childhood memories, like the comfort of an old friend.

She finally turned into a driveway between two large iron gates. The road was lined with palm trees and it wound uphill through the well-manicured estate. We came to a stop on a circular drive at the entrance to a huge white mansion. The heavy wooden doors opened as we approached, and a prim and proper butler emerged.

"Spaulding, this is Mr. Dugan," Mrs. Rigney said. "He has an appointment with R.J. this morning."

"Very good, madam," the butler responded. "Mr. Rigney is on the terrace. You may wait in the foyer, Mr. Dugan." He took my hat and coat and led me into a huge open area in the middle of the house, then disappeared.

The foyer had marble floors and immense marble columns. They went up to a high arched ceiling covered in a tile mosaic of the Greek goddess Pomona, her cornucopia brimming with freshly harvested fruits, nuts, and grains. It was a magnificent area that commanded a vast view of the entire harbor and casino.

"If you'll follow me, Mr. Rigney will see you now." I spun around. The butler waited with a bland expression. With that, Spaulding turned smartly and headed, I assumed, toward the terrace.

As I moved to follow, there came a bright, "Well, hello there," from the top of the stair landing.

I turned, and before me stood a beautiful, dark-featured young girl of around twenty. She stood in front of a large window, from which the light streaming through her thin cotton robe projected a silhouette that left little to the imagination. Firm, perky, stunning, strutting, sensual—the list of carnal adjectives danced across my lecherous brain.

As she slowly descended the staircase, the entire list that had flashed through my mind seconds ago was reaffirmed with each sensuous step. She reached the bottom of the stairs and seemed to glide across the floor to where I, without much success, tried to keep from drooling. She came close and began to slowly circle me, caressing with her eyes and body.

"You're cute," she said, her body pressed firmly to mine. "But you dress like a flatfoot."

"I'm sorry; I was going for a Shamus look," I responded.

"What's your problem?" she asked, peeling herself off my body.

"I'm a private investigator," I said.

"Oh, God, a gumshoe," she snorted, half disgusted. "Too bad." She turned and stalked away.

I watched as she disappeared down the hall then smiled, wiped the beads of perspiration forming above my upper lip, and turned to catch up with the butler. As I did, I was brought up short. Spaulding was standing sternly in front of me, looking rather annoyed.

"That's an interesting young lady," I said sheepishly. "She just gave me the frisking of a lifetime and never once used her hands."

"Yes," he said, one eyebrow lifted, signifying his displeasure. He pushed my hat, taken upon my arrival, into my chest, mercilessly crushing it flat. "Your enthusiasm is apparent. Perhaps you'll wish to carry your own hat. Now, Mr. Dugan, if you'll walk this way, Mr. Rigney is waiting." Again, he turned smartly and headed toward the terrace.

"If I could walk that way," I said under my breath, "I wouldn't need this hat."

Spaulding stopped, placed his hand in the small of his back, and displayed an unkind digit of displeasure before continuing his staunch march to the terrace. I followed with a smile.

The terrace commanded an even more magnificent view of the harbor than had the foyer. The terrace was bright and sunny and festooned with a glorious array of flowers and other topical flora.

"Mr. Dugan to see you, sir," Spaulding announced. I was forced to hurry my step in order to arrive at the proper moment.

"Very good, Spaulding," said the old man. "Please fetch us some brandy."

Before Spaulding turned to go, I asked that he also bring some coffee to go with the brandy, as it was a bit early in the morning for me.

"Yes, of course, sir," he said. And then off he went with mincing stride.

"Mr. Dugan," the old man said, "very happy to make your acquaintance, sir; please have a seat. I apologize for the accommodations afforded you. We attempted to make your arrival as inconspicuous as possible. We will have to concoct a 'cover'—I believe that is the proper vernacular of your profession—that will suit your activities ashore.

"As you will no doubt hear many times during your visit, this is a small island and news travels fast. Nothing remains a secret very long. No matter how twisted or convoluted, the facts will be disseminated. Everyone knows something about everything that occurs on this island. Whatever story we concoct will probably serve as a viable deception for only a limited period. I will leave those details to you and my daughter-in-law."

Spaulding returned with a silver serving tray, poured coffee for me and brandy for old man Rigney. He set the decanter on the table alongside the pot of coffee and returned to his duties inside.

"I don't think Spaulding approves of me," I said, pouring a sociable splash of brandy into my cup.

"Ahhhhh," laughed the old man. "Get used to it. I'm sure Spaulding has not approved of most of the behavior exhibited by the members of this family for some time.

"You see before you, Mr. Dugan, the patriarch of a family whose obsession with wealth has thoroughly corrupted each member; we indulge in a life of wicked debauchery, to which they all have become blasphemously accustomed. Ahhhh," he laughed again. "Don't get me wrong, Mr. Dugan. I have enjoyed every perverted minute of my life. But, alas, my example has not produced offspring with pure morals or strength of character. Fortunately," he continued, "the one exception to the rule is my daughter-in-law, Lara. She is a lovely, bright, intelligent woman of impeccable character. She's loyal and possesses a shrewd sense of humor and a gracious, warm heart. Lara was the best thing that ever happened to this family and the wisest decision my son Johnny ever made. Lara has an inner strength I envy. I care for her deeply and can't imagine life here without her."

After a moment of reflection, the old man seemed to snap back to the subject at hand. He downed a shot, let out a sigh of satisfaction, and slammed the glass back down on the table. He poured himself another shot, leaned back in his chair, and gazed out over his personal fiefdom, which spread to the horizon before him.

"Mr. Dugan," he finally said. "I trust my daughter-in-law implicitly. I want you to communicate your progress to Lara on a continuous basis. She's a sharp girl and possesses a vast amount of information you will find vital during the course of your endeavors.

"Let me assure you, Mr. Dugan," he said, "I am under no delusion that you will find my son alive—nor do I hold out much hope that we will ever find his remains. You see, I have lost my wife and both of my sons, and I have yet to experience the solace, or closure, that comes with the ceremony of a burial. What I do wish, however," he said as he leaned close, "is to discover what happened to my son and who is responsible."

Chapter 2

The Tour

The morning sun had risen high in the clear blue sky by the time I had concluded my meeting with "the Commodore." To Mrs. Rigney and close friends, he was R.J.; to Spaulding, other employees, and the corporate world, he was Mr. Rigney. And to the international yacht club crowd and everyone on the island, I came to find, he was the Commodore.

As I stood in the circular drive in front of the house enjoying the warm sun, Spaulding delivered a bright, shiny convertible. Engine running, top down, door open, and ready for action.

Mrs. Rigney emerged from the house. She breezed past me—sunglasses on, scarf in hand—got behind the wheel, and closed the door. She leaned out the window and pulled her sunglasses to the end of her nose. She peered from under long, delicious lashes with cattish eyes and said, "I thought you might like to get a feel for the place—the lay of the land, so to speak. Hm?"

Man, she was good. She was really good. The look, the moves—the whole package. There was something about her—from the second I heard her voice over the phone to the late-night introduction on the pier. She was terribly intriguing. An excitement stirred within me that I had never felt with this intensity with any other woman in my life. She made me feel as though I were a voyeur in a sensuous dream of her creation.

"Well?" she asked, revving the engine. I suddenly realized I had been standing, a big grin on my face, daydreaming, and twirling my hat on the end of my finger. (What a Gonzo.) I was trying to masquerade as the stuff British spy novels are made of, and instead I spun off to la-la-land and wound up looking like a starry-eyed moron. *Maybe she'll think I'm cute.*

11

I got in and closed the door. Off we sped down the winding drive and out onto the road I had come to know so well. She pegged the RPMs and shifted through the gears like a veteran European Grand Prix racer. She knew the road well and cut the apex of the inside corners like a pro. Downshifting in, a touch of the brake with the heel of her gas pedal foot, and accelerating out of the corner back through the gears. It was an intricate ballet of precision, speed, and beauty.

We headed north back across the face of the hill behind Avalon. The harbor sped past on our right, the blue Pacific beyond. On our left, the steep hill continued up to the highest peak on the island, where the airport was located. We left the harbor area and began a long descent down the hill into open country; she finally eased up on the throttle and allowed the car to move down the road at a more comfortable pace.

She smiled as I released my death grip from the seat and armrest, allowing the blood to once again flow to my knuckles. I unclenched the back of my lap and settled into the seat, enjoying the scenery as it whipped by.

"Where did you learn to drive like that?" I asked.

She looked at me, smiled, and looked back at the road. She brushed her hand through her windswept hair. "Well, not wanting to sound pretentious, let's just say that I've played with some very expensive toys in some very opulent playgrounds. Oops," she said, only slightly embarrassed, "I guess that sounded awfully pretentious anyway."

She quickly changed the subject. "That's Goat Harbor over there," she said, pointing past me and down the hill to the right. I looked over, and sure enough, a herd of goats grazed precipitously upon the steep cliff faces. "Pirates used to drop them off when they sailed these waters to insure a reliable food supply the next time they were in the area," she explained.

"I understand the Commodore was quite the rapscallion in his day," I said, in an attempt to meander to more difficult, personal questions. Slowly, with feigned contempt, she said, "Smooth segue, Dugan." So much for subtlety.

"You're right, Mrs. Rigney, I am crude and boorishly obvious. But I've been pussyfootin' around since I got here, and I still don't know much more about this case than what you originally told me over the phone. I'm not sure what it is you want me to do. Surely, the police investigated. What did they determine?"

She paused, smiling. "Pussyfootin'?" she asked. "Dugan, you don't seem to be the kind of guy who pussyfoots anywhere. Unless you count the scene in the foyer this morning with Rita."

"Yes, that was an interesting introduction," I said. "Who is Rita?"

"Rita is R.J.'s illegitimate daughter," she explained. "A rather embarrassing indiscretion with the former housekeeper. It happened many years ago. As I understand the story, the house-keeper accused R.J. of rape, and of course, R.J. not wanting an ugly, public airing of dirty laundry, paid off the housekeeper to leave the island after the birth of the baby. Since then, R.J. raised Rita as his legitimate daughter."

"And what is the relationship like between R.J. and Rita?" I asked.

"It's not a close relationship," she explained. "But none of the relationships are all that close in the family. Everyone eventually went his or her own directions. Everyone had different interests and motivations, and each possessed the means by which to pursue them. None of the family relationships were estranged, or even strained. They just gravitated to different interests. Rita is a promiscuous tease, spoiled, and has an occasional problem with the bottle. There are rumors on the island that R.J. paid a small fortune to various blackmailers over the years to keep sleazy pictures and seamy stories out of the public eye. I can't confirm the rumors, as it all happened before I met Johnny and moved to the island.

"Since I've been here," she continued, "Rita has had several boyfriends, all of whom take advantage of her in one way or another. Her latest beau is Nicky Fallon, the casino manager. He seems to treat her okay, but I don't trust him."

"Nicky Fallon?" I asked.

"Nicky was my husband Johnny's assistant, until Johnny's disappearance. Since that time, he has taken over the operation of the entire casino, including the ballroom, dining, and gambling venues. Nicky seems a nice enough guy," she said. "He's well educated, articulate, and very attractive, but he seems to have an ulterior motive. I don't know what his intentions are, and I keep him at arm's length."

"How is the ownership of the casino handled?" I asked.

"The casino, along with the other ventures on the island, such as the Catalina steamer and port facilities, is owned and operated by the Catalina Cattle Company, which itself is a wholly-owned subsidiary of the Rigney Corporation. The majority and controlling interest in the corporation is held by R.J., of course, with smaller shares controlled by other members of the immediate family."

We had reached about midway up the coast, where the road turned away from shore and began to wind to the interior. The terrain began to get a little flatter as the road traversed what seemed to be a plateau on our way to the northern end of the island.

Ahead on the road appeared several large, dark objects. Mrs. Rigney began to slow the car, until before us we saw what appeared to be...buffalo? She brought the car to a stop and allowed the beasts to cross the road at their own leisurely pace. They only occasionally acknowledged our presence with an uninterested glance or annoyed snort.

"You're not going to tell me the pirates dumped bison on the island, too, are you?" I asked.

"No," she said with a slight laugh. "Those, I'm afraid, are incantations of R.J.'s—a polite nose tweak of the proverbial Jones'. Or in this case, the Hearsts."

"As in William Randolph?" I asked.

"Yes. Shortly after Billy built that gorgeous, though ostentatious, castle on the coast at San Simeon, R.J. imported a herd of bison from Montana or some such place," she said. "Bill Hearst had his castle and thousands of acres surrounding it stocked with wild, exotic animals from Africa. R.J. has his casino and an island inhabited by buffalo."

The warm sun was still high overhead and a tropical breeze began to whip across the low, gently sloping northern end of the island.

"This is the isthmus," she said as she slowed the car on a narrow causeway separating a deep calm cove on either side, each the size of small harbors fringed with flat, white beaches.

Across the narrow causeway, the land widened again for several hundred yards, then dropped quickly to the sea at the rugged northern point. Between the isthmus causeway and the end of the island, on a wide palm covered plain, lay a neat track of white, wood-framed bungalows, each with a smokestack through the roof and a cook pot hung over an open campfire in front.

"This is Cooley Town," she said, as she slowed and turned around on the far side of the causeway. "Chinese laborers came to the island after building the railroad on the mainland to help lay the first telephone cable across the channel. After that, they went to work in the mines or to live off the sea as fishermen. As you can see by all the fishing boats in the harbors, they manage very well."

"How do the local commercial fishermen get along with the Cooley boats?" I asked.

"They don't bother each other, generally. Each fishes separate areas around the island. The commercial boats go farther out in search of halibut, bass, or tuna, while the Cooley boats ply the shallow coastal waters for octopus, squid, eel, or shellfish. They rarely encounter each other, except for the occasional squabble in the Chinese whorehouses," she said with a wicked little grin.

She put the car in gear and sped down the road on the windward side of the island, heading south. We hadn't gone far before we approached a tranquil, pale blue, shallow cove surrounded by a pristine, white beach. The cove was calm and smooth, with a warm breeze gently sweeping across long, flowing grasses that grew sparsely above the shoreline.

She drove onto the beach and turned the motor off. She opened the trunk and produced a blanket and a large wicker picnic basket. She kicked off her shoes by the car and walked out onto the beach. "I had Spaulding fix up a lunch for us," she said, as she spread the blanket and began to distribute the contents of the basket onto the blanket.

She was dressed in a khaki shorts and shirt outfit—sort of tropical safari attire from a designer runway. She sat with her long, tanned legs crossed in front of her as she poured champagne from a chilled bottle.

I lay down on the blanket across from her and propped myself up on one elbow. We touched our glasses and toasted to warm sunny days and cool evening breezes. Life was good and the world was beautiful, I thought to myself, as the sparkling bubbles danced over my tongue.

"This cove is called Little Harbor," she explained. "This is where the locals come when they want to get away from the hubbub of Avalon. It's one of the most serene spots on the island."

We casually ate the lunch Spaulding had prepared, enjoying each other's company and the warm, sunny day. It was a scrumptious buffet of pate finger sandwiches, caviar and crackers, cheese wedges and apple slices.

I lay on my back, my arm cradling my head, gazing up into a bright clear sky.

"I don't think I ever want to leave this spot," I said. "It must be wonderful living on the island."

She rolled over on her stomach, propping herself up on her elbows, holding the champagne glass in both hands and gently caressing it with her sumptuous lips. "I fell in love with the island the moment I stepped ashore," she said with a dreamy sigh. "I was a night club singer. I'd bounced around all the clubs from L.A. to New York and back. I'd been around the world as a torch song ballad singer on cruise shops when I landed here. I came to the island to sing at the ballroom in the casino with the Mickey Dora Orchestra. That's how I met Johnny." Her voice trailed off, and she fell silent for a time.

"Dugan," she finally said, "you mentioned earlier that you didn't understand why I asked you to come or what I wanted you to do. I'm not sure myself. I don't know what else to do, or where else to turn. Not just for me, but for R.J. He's lost so much in the last few years, and there's just nothing but emptiness in the old man's soul. For a man who has lived such a rich, full life—to have that life become a hollow shell of lonely memories is just too heartbreaking for me to bear. He and I both need to heal the open wound we carry in our hearts. Close this chapter in our lives and move on. We need to find out what happened to Johnny."

"You must have loved him very much?" I asked softly.

She paused for a moment, staring into the glass of rising bubbles. "It wasn't an all-consuming, passion-fired sort of love," she said. "It was a warm, secure, comfortable love that we both seemed to settle into, the type of love that grows over time—matures like a fine wine, or a sturdy oak tree. I think it was something both of us secretly yearned for and were lucky enough to have found it in each other."

She fell silent again for a time. Finally, she began to clear the blanket and return the accoutrements of lunch back to the basket. We went back to the car, and put the basket and blanket in the trunk. We got in and headed south, down the windward side of the island. Again, the blue Pacific was on our right, and the rugged hills rose abruptly on our left.

This side of the island was much steeper than was the other, and the cliffs dropped sharply to the crashing surf. The road seemed to hang precariously over the side of the cliffs, and terrain was stark and rugged.

"You wanted to know what the authorities came up with during the course of their investigation into Johnny's disappearance?" she asked. "Virtually nothing," she answered. Chief Constable LaFarge and his staff pieced together the sequence of events up until Johnny headed out to sea. It wasn't much more than we already knew by talking to the harbormaster and other fishermen around the docks.

"Johnny was going marlin fishing in the morning," she continued. "He and Miguel, the man who took care of the boat for Johnny, left the harbor early in the morning under bright sunny skies and calm seas. They were never seen again. No trace of them or the boat has ever been found. And the answer to your next obvious questions," she said, "is no. I don't know of anyone that would want something to happen to Johnny. I don't know of anyone who would want him dead."

Her voice quivered and trailed off. She wiped away a tear from under her dark glasses. She quietly regained her composure. "I'm sorry, Dugan," she said, "but I just realized that that was the first time I have spoken of Johnny as being dead, rather than missing. I'm sorry; I wasn't quite ready for that. It kind of snuck up on me."

We drove along in silence for a while. I was beginning to realize what the Commodore felt when he spoke to Lara's compassion and strength. Though she bore a heavy burden and at times was timid and vulnerable, she carried on with her head up, proud, self-reliant, and gracious.

We continued south down the narrow winding road until we approached what appeared to be some sort of large excavation or mining operation to the right, on the side of the steep hillside, at the water's edge.

A large conveyor emerged from a cave or mine within the cliff and deposited a dry, light, sandy material in a huge pile near the beach. A steam shovel then loaded it onto a large, flat barge towed by a tug.

"What is that?" I asked.

"That's a bat guano mining operation," she answered.

"You're kidding?" I said in disbelief.

"No," she assured me. "Bat guano is very high in phosphates and nitrates. It's used in everything from fertilizers to pharmaceuticals, and there are limited sources from which the process of extracting the material is a profitable venture. Other sources of bat guano, with a few exceptions, are deep in inaccessible jungles or through terrain too rugged to feasibly transport the product to a shipping point. This is one of the larger deposits in the known world, and it is relatively easy to extract and load onto barges for shipping to the mainland."

"Is this operation run by the Catalina Cattle Company also?" I asked.

"No," she said. "The land is leased to the mining company with a percentage paid in the form of royalties, based upon tonnage of material extracted. It's the same arrangement as for the rock quarry on the other side of the island. We'll see that when we pass Seal Rock, around the point on the other side—south of Avalon. The area down where the mining is conducted is known as Smuggler's Cove, and the outcropping of land ahead is called China Point.

"The cove was used extensively by smugglers and bootleggers during prohibition," she explained. "Legend has it that R.J., in cahoots with Joe Kennedy, made a fortune smuggling Scotch from the Kennedy compound in Hyannis Port through the Panama Canal and off-loaded here for distribution all along the west coast. The deep cove," she continued, "made for easy delivery to the beach, and the bat cave was ideal for safekeeping until distribution to the mainland. China Point shelters the cove during rough seas and provides an excellent lookout for the Coast Guard or other marauding pirates."

"You certainly seem to know a lot about the history of the island," I said.

"It's a small island, Dugan. Catalina has a rich history of mystery and intrigue. Much of that intrigue centers on the Rigney family, so it's only natural that I know some of the more interesting tales. Besides," she continued, "it makes for great party banter at the European pooh-pooh balls and embassy cocktail parties. Oops, there I go sounding pretentious again." She leaned over playfully and said, "I want you to pinch me the next time I say something like that, okay? I don't want it to become a habit with me."

"I promise I'll sound the fathead alarm the next time you try to blue-nose somebody," I answered with a smile.

By this time, we had descended China Point and were rounding the southern end of the island. Down to the right, in the middle of another pale-blue, serene cove, emerged an immense rock covered with sea lions bathing themselves in the warm afternoon sun. The cove had a white sand bottom clearly visible through the crystalline water that gently rose to an equally pristine white beach. The beach was also covered with slumbering sea lions, which only occasionally shooed away a pesky fly, or casually scratched an itch with a sandy fin. It looked like siesta time at Seal Rock.

After we passed Seal Rock, the road again climbed steeply, high over the Pacific and up to the top of the rugged peak before us. Once we reached the top, the view was spectacular, but disconcerting. A person suffering from vertigo would find the sight of the sheer drop to the craggy shore below very uncomfortable.

Ahead, far down the slope near the beach, was another mining operation. This was an open-pit mine that gouged out the side of the mountain and deposited huge, granite boulders on the beach, where again, a steam shovel loaded them onto a large, flat barge in tow by tug.

"The boulders they remove from the quarry," she explained, "are towed to the mainland for the construction of breakwaters, jetties, and marinas along the southern California coast. Again, because of the ease of access and proximity to shipping facilities, this operation is unique and therefore regarded as perhaps the most desirable location from which to obtain this material. The characteristics of Catalina rock also make them the best."

"Which means what?" I asked.

"Which means," she explained with a hardy laugh, "to be good, it has to be big and hard. That looks like Captain Wally's boat down there. You remember Captain Wally, don't you?"

"Yes, I remember him," I said. "He's quite a character."

"He used to be the skipper of the *Lucky Dutchman*, R.J.'s yacht, when he still used it. Before the accident," she said.

"Accident?" I asked.

"Yes," she explained. "You remember R.J. telling you that he lost his wife and both sons? It happened before I came to the island. R.J., his wife Natalie, and a well-known Hollywood film director were on the boat one night, moored down by the isthmus. R.J. and the director were having a heated argument— something to do with an indiscreet liaison that supposedly occurred between Natalie and the director. Sometime that evening, Mrs. Rigney went out on deck, leaving the men to their argument. She was never seen or heard from again.

"Of course, a massive search was undertaken, but there was never a trace. The only thing they ever found was the ship's dinghy bobbing in the surf line down by Land's End at the northern tip of the island. R.J. has never set foot on the boat again," she said. "He keeps it at a private mooring just down from the estate next to the boathouse, where the speed boat is kept."

"What about the other son?" I asked.

"P.K. is the older of the two boys," she explained. "He was somewhat of a rogue, an adventurer. P.K. was lost while on a treasure hunt near the East China Sea, off the western islands of Japan. Some believe pirates attacked his boat, and he was killed and thrown overboard. Again," she said, "no trace was ever found. That is why we need your help, Dugan. We need to find out what happened to Johnny. There may be some connection between the deaths, or maybe a horrible curse has befallen this family. I can't imagine any of this being connected, but whatever the whys or hows, I hope you can find some answers."

We crested the top of the mountain and began a steep, winding descent down the narrow road precariously etched into the side of the rugged cliff. I tried to assimilate all the information Mrs. Rigney had poured out during our tour and keep my mind off the incredible vertical drop that loomed to the right, just inches from the edge of the road.

It was an intriguing story she had laid out. I, too, could not imagine how any of the family's misfortunes could conceivably relate to each other. They weren't even coincidences; the events occurred years apart, and in P.K.'s case, in an entirely different part of the world. They seemed totally separate incidents. I believed I should concentrate on Johnny's disappearance, to the exclusion of all other misfortunes.

Suddenly, a black sedan roared up behind us from out of nowhere. It smashed into the rear of our roadster and pushed us down the steep narrow road toward a sharp left curve. With much difficulty, Lara managed to keep us on the road, but the sedan was relentless, and we hurtled toward the curve, scraping hard against the cliff on our left, then being thrown back out toward the edge of the road on our right.

She downshifted and punched the accelerator, attempting to pull away from the sedan and regain control. We pulled away long enough to make the curve, but the sedan was just inches behind. Repeatedly, the sedan smashed into the rear of the roadster, attempting to run us off the road. When we came to a short straightaway, the sedan tried to pull alongside.

"Don't let him get next to us," I yelled. "He'll shove us over the side."

She stomped the gas pedal, and the little red roaster jumped ahead of our pursuer, in a grotesque, granite bobsled nightmare—a roller coaster ride to hell.

I gripped the seat hard and contorted as the sedan rammed us again, sending us into the jagged cliff on our left. Showers of sparks exploded from the side of the car as metal tore away and the roadster was dashed to the other side of the road, careening off a stone barrier that kept us from plunging to the crashing surf below.

"Do something," she cried. "I can't keep him off of us." She worked the pedals frantically, brake to gas, downshift, and then back on the gas. Her arms sawed the steering wheel back and forth, but the sedan stayed glued to our bumper. The view out the back of the roadster was the chrome grill of the big black sedan.

I looked ahead; another short straightaway was upon us. She jammed the accelerator to the floor and the roadster gained a few precious inches. I pulled my .38 from its holster under my left armpit and put four shots through the driver's side windshield of the sedan. The sedan instantly veered right and plunged over the cliff. It fell for what seemed an eternity, until finally impacting on the jagged rocks halfway down the cliff face. It exploded into a huge ball of fire, raining pieces of flaming metal down the cliff and into the thrashing surf.

I holstered my rod and turned to Lara, who was still fighting for control of the car.

"Okay, he's gone," I said. "You can slow down now."

"I wish I could," she responded. "We have no brakes."

I looked down; she was frantically pumping the pedal in a feeble attempt to slow the runaway car. It had no effect. The pedal went to the floorboards, and the roadster continued to hurtle down the narrow road, gaining momentum.

"I hope you can swim," she said. "Cause we're not going to make the curve at Lover's Cove."

We careened down the road at breakneck speed with the sharp left curve looming before us. She put the car into the side of the hill, attempting to slow us down. Shards of metal were ripped from the side of the car, and the grinding sounds of a train wreck exploded all around.

"Get ready," she yelled. "Don't jump until we go over the side and clear the rocks below."

She steered the car away from the hill and aimed it toward the horizon directly ahead. As the car left the road and flew into the air, everything became perfectly silent. We seemed to float

23

through the air in slow motion as the car began to dive toward the Pacific.

"Now," she screamed, and we ejected ourselves from the top of the car just before it plunged into the sea.

I pulled my knees up to my chest and tucked my head, hitting the water like a cannonball. The force with which I hit knocked the wind out of me for a few seconds. I went limp and allowed the swirling bubbles to carry me back to the surface. I lifted my head above the surface and took a deep breath then performed a quick inventory and determined that all my parts had remained attached, though I was beginning to get sore.

I regained my senses and frantically began searching the churning water for Lara. I called and called, swimming in circles, desperately searching for any sign of her. I had finally decided to dive down to the submerging roadster before it was too late when she exploded from beneath the water, gasping for air. I quickly swam to where she floated on the surface, her chest heaving in an attempt to regain her breath.

"Are you all right, angel?" I asked.

"I don't know," she said. "I can't move; I'm numb."

I grabbed the back of her shirt collar and began sidestroking toward shore. I swam as quickly as I could, praying that she was all right. I reached the beach, exhausted, and dragged her and myself onto the sand. We lay there for a while, trying to regain our senses.

Finally, she wiped her wet, bedraggled hair from her face and raised herself to one knee. She turned toward me and said, "I'm sure glad we had the top down. It would have been a real bitch getting out, otherwise." We began to giggle hysterically in fright, shock, and relief. We had survived.

Chapter 3

The Ball

Just before sunset, we walked the short distance down the beach to the Rigneys' boathouse. Form there we called Spaulding, who picked us up and drove us back to the estate.

They deposited me in the guesthouse adjacent to the servant's quarters at the rear of the estate. While I showered and shaved, Spaulding retrieved my soggy pile of wet clothes and replaced them with an entire evening wardrobe, including a white dinner jacket that fit better than anything I had ever owned.

Mrs. Rigney and I were to attend the grand ball at the casino that evening. The ball was the beginning of an annual, week-long cultural bazaar that attracted art dealers and connoisseurs from around the globe. According to Mrs. Rigney, the bazaar was the inaugural event of the globetrotting social season. Tonight, I would mingle with the international "hoity-toity" and haute couture, the hip and the hangers-on. I had been dutifully advised by Spaulding to curtail my de's and doe's and youse-guys during my foray into the realm of the educated, sophisticated, and articulate. Spaulding. I have to admit that I liked the pompous ass, but he was an affected jerk.

I instructed Spaulding to summon a cab for Mrs. Rigney and me, rather than having him drive us to the ball. I also requested that he stay in the mansion with R.J. and have Manuel, the groundskeeper, close the iron gates after we left and periodically check the estate during the evening. I wanted the estate to be secure until Mrs. Rigney and I returned from the ball. I was not at all satisfied with the security arrangements, but it was the best we could do for tonight.

I finished dressing and made my way across the courtyard to the entrance of the mansion. As I arrived at the front doors, they opened, and out walked a goddess in gold satin. The stunning apparition that appeared before me in the moonlight overwhelmed me. She was the most gorgeous creature I had ever seen. The gown flowed over her firm body like liquid gold, and her untethered figure moved tautly beneath the thin silk robe. Her long, auburn hair cascaded about her shoulders, and her eyes—her eyes were deep pools of sensual ebony. I was awestruck. I was paralyzed. Spaulding walked up to me and with great relish, playfully slapped me across the kisser, bringing me back to my senses.

"Thanks, I needed that," I said.

He smiled and replied, "Oh, my pleasure, sir. Any time."

The cab arrived, and we drove down the hill to the casino. On the ride downtown, Mrs. Rigney informed me that we were to meet a Mr. Harold Peters at the ball. I couldn't help but laugh.

"We're going to the ball to meet Harry Peters?" I asked.

The cabbie laughed, she slapped me across the knee and jokingly told me not to act like that when we got to the party.

"That's twice that I've been slapped tonight, and I haven't even gotten to the party yet," I said. "This should be a real fun evening."

We arrived at the glittering palace amid throngs of immaculately coiffed, splendidly attired guests. The beautiful people. The privileged. The rich. The pampered. With each new arrival, the paparazzi scrambled in mass confusion and flash bulbs.

The hectic exuberance out front was in stark contrast to the magnificent elegance that surrounded us upon entering the spacious ballroom. The ballroom was an immense area illuminated by spectacular crystal chandeliers suspended from a radiant ceiling that seemed to twinkle like the canopy of the night's own stars. The floor was a dark, highly polished black walnut that extended outward in a radiant pattern to the walls, where huge arched columns, also of black walnut, supported the ceiling and gaming room above, without any supporting pillars in the interior of the open ballroom. It was an impressive bit of engineering.

The walls of the room were a continuous underwater mural in art deco style. The entire expanse of the magnificent ballroom was a luminous fantasy palace. It was difficult to imagine that something this beautiful was actually real. Much the same feeling I got when I gazed at the gorgeous piece of glossy architecture accompanying me to the ball.

Across the dance floor, opposite the entrance to the ballroom, was an immense stage, upon which played the orchestra. To the left was a grand and intricately carved bar, complete with hustling tenders and eager patrons. The remainder of the room was filled with elegantly decorated dining tables that followed the design of the room in a circular pattern around the dazzling dance floor. It was an impressive structure and deserving of the accolades of everyone who had experienced the pleasure of its scope and ambiance. The entire room was a beehive of activity—diners, dancers, scurrying waiters and waitresses, cocktail toting partygoers, and assorted entourage. It was a surreal carnival of elegance and bourgeoisie.

As we entered the room, all eyes turned to the stunning beauty I was escorting. Eyes popped and jaws dropped. The entire room fell silent when the sensual vision floated across the floor. I obviously wasn't the only person paralyzed by her beauty. If Spaulding were here, he'd have to make rounds slapping everybody back from dreamland. With each luxurious stride, the slit up the front of her gown exposed long shapely legs, almost to the top of her thighs. She was a heart-stopping vision of unparalleled beauty.

An exuberant maître d' escorted Mrs. Rigney and me to a table across from the bar and dance floor. He helped Mrs. Rigney with her chair, offered us menus, and invited us to enjoy a cocktail before we dined. Mrs. Rigney ordered champagne and requested a light for the cigarette she placed between her luscious, pouty lips. The maître d' produced a lighter from his pocket, lit her cigarette as requested, and returned the lighter to his pocket before excusing himself and returning to his duties.

"This is a spectacular structure," I said. "The Commodore must be very proud."

"Yes, I'm glad you like it," she replied. "R.J. envisioned Avalon as the cultural Mecca of the west. He wanted to create an exceptional destination for the world's elite. I think the casino is the crowning glory of that vision. It provides an alluring showcase of Catalina and a romantic atmosphere for international cultural events presented on the island. It's a very special place."

She began to hum along with the tune as the orchestra played.

"Would you care to dance?" I asked.

"I thought you'd never ask."

We crossed the dance floor, and I took her in my arms. As we danced, it seemed as though we were the only two people on the floor. She felt wonderful and exciting close to me, and we drifted across the dance floor with not a care in the world.

"I'm not very good at this," I said, "but I certainly enjoy holding you close."

"Yes, I'm beginning to realize that," she said with a curious smile. "Can't you control your emotions?"

"Perhaps we should step outside for some cool air," I suggested.

"My emotion tends to have a mind of its own."

"Well, then, perhaps we should step to the bar so I can spritz a little seltzer-water on your lust," she retorted. "Maybe that will change its train of thought."

"Keep that thought," I said. "Perhaps after the dance."

She smiled the smile I had come to know and love. She was a great sport. "Just follow me back to the table," she said. "Stay close; I'll cover you."

We returned to the table as the champagne arrived. I adroitly popped the cork and began to pour, and Mrs. Rigney informed me that Chief Constable LaFarge had arrived and was heading in our direction.

Inspector LaFarge was a tall, polished officer with rigid posture and a confident stride, severely tailored in a sharply creased uniform. He had dark, straight hair combed back, and a meticulously groomed pencil mustache. He carried his flattop legionnaire cap tucked smartly under his arm, and the bandoleer holster gave him the air of a roguish, debonair military commander of dubious affiliation. The only accessories lacking were knee-high riding boots and matching crop or expensive leather gloves that he could ceremoniously remove finger by finger upon his arrival. I think he thought he was Rudolph Valentino, matinee idol.

He strode to our table, clicked his heels together, and bowed smartly. "Good evening, Mrs. Rigney," he said. "How wonderful it is to see you. May I say how positively ravishing you look tonight?" He extended his hand and took hers, upon which he placed a chivalrous kiss. How positively continental, I thought sarcastically to myself.

"Thank you, Inspector LaFarge," she replied. "I would like you to meet my escort for the evening, Mr. Travis Dugan."

"Very happy to make your acquaintance," he said as we shook hands. "You're a fortunate man to have such a lovely guest for dinner, Mr. Dugan. I must admit, I envy you, sir."

"Would you care to join us for a glass of champagne?" Mrs. Rigney asked.

"Thank you, Mrs. Rigney," he replied. "That's very kind of you." He snapped his fingers and motioned for a waiter. He seated himself and offered each of us a cigarette from his silver case. Mrs. Rigney accepted the cigarette and the light with which he lit hers, as well as his own. He held the cigarette between his thumb and index finger, European style. How gallant, I again thought to myself sarcastically. This guy is really full of it.

The waiter arrived with another glass for the inspector and poured from the chilled bottle. The good inspector sipped politely then turned his attentions to Mrs. Rigney. "Mrs. Rigney," he began, "I cannot tell you how relieved I am that you were not harmed during this afternoon's unfortunate incident. Very distressing."

"I appreciate your sincere concern, Constable LaFarge," she replied. "However, I can assure you that Mr. Dugan and I, while a little shaken-up, are just fine and looking forward to a wonderful evening."

"I am very relieved to hear that, Mrs. Rigney," he said. "It is fortunate that Mr. Dugan was able to assist you in your time of need."

LaFarge then shifted his attention toward yours truly. "Tell me, Mr. Dugan," he began. "What brings you to our peaceful oasis?"

His face, while friendly and smiling, was perhaps too much so, and his tone a bit condescending, his eyes cold and calculating, dark and penetrating. He looked deep into my eyes, searching for any hesitation or lack of commitment. I would have to be very careful about how I responded to Chief Inspector LaFarge.

We stared at each other for maybe one uncomfortable moment too long before Mrs. Rigney broke the slowly building tension.

"Mr. Dugan has been retained by the Rigney Corporation to assist in the audit of the Catalina Cattle Company's records," she said.

Still fixated on me, the good inspector replied, "I see. Perhaps Mr. Dugan would be so kind as to come down to headquarters and provide us with a formal statement regarding today's misfortune. At your convenience, of course, Mr. Dugan."

I, too, looked intently at the inspector, lifting my champagne glass. "Yes, that would be fine," I replied.

"Have you learned anything about the person who tried to run us off the road?" asked Mrs. Rigney, attempting to divert attention from the tedious Mexican standoff in which the inspector and I were engaged. LaFarge eventually turned to Mrs. Rigney. (Stalemate terminated)

"Unfortunately, there is not much remaining of the sedan," he said. "Scattered debris strewn down the cliff face. Perhaps we will find something of significance in the morning. Darkness arrived before we could thoroughly search the waters' edge. Hopefully, tomorrow we will be able to remove your automobile from the grotto. Imagine the tourists' surprise aboard the glass-bottom boat when they peer through the glass into the interior of your roadster. I understand that a rather territorial garibaldi has staked a claim to it."

"I'm sorry we created such a problem, Inspector LaFarge," Mrs. Rigney said. "I know how busy you must be this week, with the influx of people on the island and the upcoming cultural events."

"Please, do not apologize, Mrs. Rigney," he said. "My primary concern is for your safety. That is why," he continued, "I have taken the liberty of posting one of my men outside your estate. For my own peace of mind, as well as yours."

"That's very comforting, Inspector," she replied. "Again, I deeply appreciate your concern."

"Well, then, I shall leave you to enjoy your evening," he said, as he stood. "If you will excuse me, I shall get on with my duties." He again clicked his heels together, kissed the lady's hand, and bid us a good evening. "It was a pleasure meeting you, Mr. Dugan. I look forward to seeing you tomorrow. Shall we say eleven?"

"Eleven would be fine," I replied. With that, the good inspector about-faced and was off.

"What was that all about?" she asked.

"You mean the stare down between the indomitable inspector and me? I do believe the stern constable is very suspicious of my presence. I'm not at all sure that he bought the story about the audit. He'll probably have some very pointed questions for me tomorrow. I'm expecting a less-than-friendly inquisition."

At that moment, a cadre of waiters descended upon our table. With the precision of a military invasion, they assembled the provisions upon which we would advance—locally caught lobster drowning in melted butter, baked potato likewise drowning in sour cream and chives, and broccoli smothered in a creamy hollandaise sauce. I could feel my arteries clogging before my attendant could get one of those sissy bibs tied around my neck. I was famished, having had nothing but a salt-water douche since our picnic lunch this afternoon and was elbow-deep in lobster and melted butter before Mrs. Rigney even got started. But once she did, she was no pansy in the chow line. Conversation was reduced to gratuitous grunts and ecstasy-induced sighs.

We had finished our meal and were enjoying coffee and a cigarette when a studious-looking, short, round, melon-faced nebbish approached our table. His heavy lidded eyes bulged slightly and were spread wide on his pale face. He had thin-pursed lips and the demeanor of an oft-whipped cocker spaniel. He hesitantly approached, umbrella and soft briefcase held in front, as if one would imagine a schoolboy called to the principal's office for adolescent misbehavior.

"Excuse me," he said, almost inaudibly. "I apologize for interrupting your meal. Allow me to introduce myself. I am Harold Peters. I have been assigned the audit of the Catalina Cattle Company."

"Ah, yes, Mr. Peters," she replied. "I'm Lara Rigney. We've been expecting you. Please join us for refreshments."

"Thank you, Mrs. Rigney," he said as he gingerly seated himself. "That is very gracious of you."

"Mr. Peters, I'd like you to meet Mr. Dugan," she said. "He'll be assisting you—recovering misplaced documents, locating inventory, searching official records, etcetera."

"A pleasure to make your acquaintance, Mr. Dugan," he said. He spoke in an odd, pronounced whisper, almost as if he were perpetually out of breath. "It is rare that I enjoy the luxury of an assistant; however, I assure you, it will be greatly appreciated. Perhaps together we might expedite this task with minimal delay."

"Glad to meet you Harry," I said. "Looking forward to working with you. Can I buy you a drink?"

"Well, perhaps I could trouble you for a brandy," he said.

"Excellent suggestion, Harry. I think we all could go for a brandy." I motioned for the waiter and placed our request.

"I trust your passage was satisfactory, Mr. Peters?" Lara asked.

"Well, I'm not much of a seaman," he replied, "but it was a calm and pleasant voyage."

"I arranged accommodations for you at the Glenmore," Mrs. Rigney said. "A quaint Victorian just up the street. You can pick up your room key from the desk clerk; they're expecting you."

"That is very kind of you, Mrs. Rigney. I'm sure I will be very comfortable. I must compliment you on the inspiring series of events taking place on this lovely island and the magnificence of the casino."

"Thank you, Mr. Peters," she said. "I hope you find the time to enjoy some of the island's other pleasures during your stay."

The brandy arrived, and we toasted to a successful week of festivities. The orchestra played, and the gleaming dance floor was a swirl of elegant gowns and glittering lights. A never-ending parade of well-wishers and wannabes made their obligatory appearance in the presence of the princess of the island ball. Octogenarian aristocracy, the island's social elite, Old World money, and the nouveau riche paid their respects to the representative of the island's reigning monarchy. Perhaps I am a bit harsh, but I was tired of all the polite chitchat. So much to-do about nothing. I've never really been much of a schmoozer.

It was all more or less a load of trite BS as far as I was concerned. A pinky waving colossal waste of time. I usually attended functions such as this only on rare occasions, to scout the territory for rich, bored "debu-tramps" in need of ebullient escapades. Oh, well. It's a tough job, but somebody has to do it.

We swirled and swished brandy for what seemed an eternity amid a continuing procession of brownnosers and social suckups salivating over every minute detail of our afternoon sojourn and enigmatic splashdown into Lover's Cove. After the umpteenth repetition of the story and an almost endless exchange of shallow pleasantries and insipid advancing claustrophobia, Mrs. Rigney suggested we adjourn to the upstairs casino, where we might be introduced to the always-charming Nicky Fallon, casino manager extraordinaire.

The stairway to the casino was a magnificent hand-carved black walnut of art deco design, inlaid with liberal amounts of gold leaf. The plushly carpeted, gilded path was cantilevered out from the circular wall, and rose up and over the bar to the left of the ballroom. The heavenly ascent afforded a spectacular view of the room below.

I gallantly insisted that Mr. Peters and Mrs. Rigney precede me as we climbed the intricately designed, ornate stairway while I took up the rear, so to speak. And what a rear it was. My undaunted chivalry allowed for an unobstructed observation of Mrs. Rigney's firm and supple derriere, which quivered ever so slightly with each enchanting step. The muscles of her tanned, sculptured legs rippled tautly, and her body created sensuous patterns beneath a gown that flowed like windswept fields of golden wheat. She teasingly accentuated her sway and looked back occasionally with a flirtatious grin, knowing full well that I was enjoying our stroll upstairs almost as much as I had enjoyed our dance.

The casino was an immense wonderland of glitz and glamour. The architecture and décor were similar to the ballroom—richly polished walnut beams extending to a domed ceiling, from which hung enormous crystal chandeliers. In the ballroom, the walls were submarine art deco murals, but in the casino, the walls were huge sheets of plate glass incorporating a three hundred and sixty-degree view of the harbor, city, and blue Pacific. Outside, through glass doors, was an open balcony that circled the entire second floor. The integration of structure and environment created a romantic intimacy between the harbor and the natural beauty of the surrounding island. You dreamed of sailing away to places such as this on warm, lazy summer afternoons. The smell of fresh mowed grass. The feel of soft summer breezes. You dreamed of falling in love with a place such as this. You dreamed of a place such as this in which to fall in love.

Chapter 4

Our Host

Nicky Fallon was the poster boy for tall, dark, and handsome. The title fit him like a glove in the immaculate white dinner jacket that adorned his athletic, well-tanned physique. He was a matinee idol, an Adonis in patent leather Florsheims. It was no wonder that everybody, but mostly women, seemed to gravitate to whatever space he happened to be occupying and orbit his magnetic personal charm. I couldn't help but envy the bastard. (I hate when that happens.) The gorgeous s.o.b. was everything we wished we were. He, of course, was captain of the football team and boinked all the comely cheerleaders after the big game. He was class president and homecoming king. He had the world's loveliest bounty laid at his feet for him to pick and choose at his whim—the ripest fruit from the finest orchards, the softest and most radiant of flowers from the kingdom's richest gardens. He seemed a lucky guy with very little effort expended, and thoroughly enjoyed every luscious, damn moment of it, too.

Nicky Fallon was engaged in amorous banter with a bevy of young, shiny nymphs, all bouncy and bubbly. When he spotted Mrs. Rigney et al, he politely extricated himself from the disappointed puerile kittens and hastened to greet his guests.

"Lara," he said intimately, "you look radiant this evening, as always." He took her hand in both of his, leaned forward, and placed a lingering kiss upon her cheek. "I'm happy that you're all right and pleased that you're able to join us this evening. I was terribly distressed to hear of your misfortune."

Mrs. Rigney assured him that all was well and proceeded to introduce Mr. Peters and myself.

"Nicky Fallon, I'd like you to meet Mr. Peters and Mr. Dugan. Mr. Peters will be conducting the audit that I told you about, and Mr. Dugan will be assisting."

"Gentlemen, it's a pleasure to make your acquaintance," he said sincerely. "My staff and I are eager to assist you in your endeavors in any way we can. Please, don't hesitate to call on us at anytime. The maintenance staff arrives at seven AM, and the office and bookkeeping staff arrive at nine. You may enter through the employee entrance on the north side of the casino, and we have provided an office, equipment, and supplies for your convenience."

Mr. Peters seemed eager to begin and asked if he might inspect the accommodations provided.

"Of course, Mr. Peters," Nicky said. "Come right this way. I'll be happy to give you the fifty-cent tour. Would you like to come along, Mr. Dugan?" he asked.

"No, thank you," I replied. "I believe I'll just wander around a bit. Perhaps I'll buy Mrs. Rigney a drink at the bar."

"Order whatever you like," he said. "It's on the house." With that, Nicky Fallon and Mr. Peters left to explore the working arrangements.

Mrs. Rigney and I strolled to the bar, and I ordered a toddy. I scanned the gaming room and menagerie of assorted guests and gamers. Again, a trickle of acquaintances began to converge upon our lovely hostess. Many, I gathered, were old friends from the far reaches of the galaxy. Each respectively insisted that Mrs. Rigney come to this extravaganza or that social engagement in other exotic locales throughout the globe.

As I lingered over my refreshment and acknowledged each new arrival with a nod or smile, I noticed a gathering of excited spectators at the baccarat table. I excused myself, though nobody noticed, and wandered over to the ensuing hubbub.

Seated at the far side of the table was a dapper, roguish middle-aged gentleman. Across from him was an older man, very round and rather jolly looking, though at the moment, intent on the game in progress.

Though I know virtually nothing about baccarat, at first glance it seemed to me that the younger man was in command of the proceedings, in that he maintained a subdued confidence. That is to say, he had a cat-eating grin on his face that seemed to pique his opponent no end. His adversary, the fat man across the table, on the other hand, was ensconced in intense concentration on the shoe containing the playing cards and passed to the confident gent across from him. The younger man slowly, and with deliberate dramatics, drew the next card, or chit, as they were called, from the shoe. A collective hush fell over the gathered spectators as the chit was revealed and tossed to the middle of the table. A cascade of oohs and ahhs came forth from the assembled masses, signifying a decisive victory for the confident, dapper young man. His rival began to flush around the collar. His jaws clenched, and he wiped his perspiring dome with his pocket kerchief, trying unsuccessfully to mask his displeasure. After a few brief moments, his flustered glow subsided, and a wide smile formed on his ample face.

"Congratulations, my friend," said the fat man, offering his hand across the table. "You proved an admirable and more than worthy opponent. I commend your shrewd and stealthy tactics. I enjoy the intensity and exhilaration of the battle. Surely I do." He barked a boisterous, hearty laugh.

"I, too, enjoyed the challenge," replied the young rival. "I look forward to a rematch."

"Excellent, excellent," retorted the fat man. "Perhaps I might extract a meager portion of revenge in our next encounter. I look forward to another contest, my victorious comrade. Surely I do."

With that, the throng of spectators dispersed, adjourning to the bar for a round of welcome refreshments. The fat man remained at the baccarat table and ordered a drink. He motioned for his companion, a huge Chinese gentleman, to lean close while the fat man whispered something into his ear. The gargantuan made no distinguishable reply or gesture. He simply turned and plodded from the room.

Both contestants, the rotund one and his dashing opponent, spoke with decidedly British accents; therefore, I deduced, through my keen sense of logic and my mental dexterity, that they were Englishmen. What profundity, what depth. That's why I get the big money.

I casually strolled around the immense room, taking in the exhilarated abandon displayed in the adult play land. It was a warm evening, and the twinkling lights from the many boats moored in the harbor reflected serenely off the calm, smooth water. The glorious view from the casino could have been Rio, or even Monte Carlo. It was a magnificent display of a festive locale vibrant with opulent fortuity.

I eventually found my way back to the bar, as is oft my modus operandi, and planted myself on one of the few unoccupied stools. I could see Mrs. Rigney through the animated gathering, still enthralled in globetrotting schedules—something about African safaris and World Cup sailboat regattas. The social agendas were gathering steam. This season apparently was to be a whirlwind carnival to rival all past seasons. Must be nice.

Just then, to my libidinous surprise, from across the room strode the ever-luscious Rita Rigney. She seemed to have a set course and maneuvered through the swirling masses with steadfast bearing, heading straight for my erection—I mean, in my direction. She wore a slithery black silk slip-dress that danced deliciously in the lights. The dress was sheer and flowing, low-cut in the front, suspended from smooth tan shoulders by thin straps that seductively slipped from her shoulders and slid down her arms. The long slit at the front of the dress exposed lithe, dark legs with every graceful stride.

She arrived to where I sat quivering with anticipation, placed both hands on my knee, leaned close, and kissed me softly on the lips. When she leaned forward to kiss me, the top of her dress softly billowed away from her body, exposing luscious caramel breasts and smooth chocolate nipples. Mouth-watering. Her skin was as smooth as a silk kimono, and around her drifted the fragrance of lilacs on a spring day. I made no attempt to maintain eye contact, as that would have been, though chivalrous, a frustrating and futile effort, and a seeming rebuff of her warm and friendly gesture. Instead, I allowed myself a long, lingering gaze that set my blood racing and heart pounding. The coy smile left no doubt that this was a private exhibition for the primal arousal of me and mine.

"Are you enjoying yourself this evening, Travis?" she asked with a smile.

"I must confess, I was beginning to get bored," I replied, "but things are looking up."

"Yes, I noticed," she said, glancing down seductively. She moved to the side, away from the bar, shielding our growing passion from the surrounding crowd. She slowly slid her hand along my thigh until she came upon "Thor, guardian of the family jewels." She was a confident traveler and had a firm grasp of the situation. She moved her body closer until her creamy thigh came to rest warmly upon my hand, which gripped the edge of the bar stool. She moved her tender body ever so slightly, allowing me to caress the warm softness of her thighs. The tension built to blinding passion. I wanted her, and I wanted her badly.

"Would you care to dance?" she whispered softly.

I sat momentarily stunned. Not quite sure what she was suggesting, or what my response should be. Whatever she offered, I was accepting with a smile.

"You do know how to dance don't you, Trav?" she cooed. "You just put your bodies together and fffflllloooow."

Salacious thoughts overwhelmed me, though I fought not to be obvious.

She gently removed my hand from her inner thigh and led me to the small dance floor across from the bar, next to the huge windows overlooking the harbor. We were the only people on the floor; the throng of gamers was engaged in the sins of wager. She held me firmly, cradling her head on my shoulder, softly nuzzling my neck. My free hand roamed the exquisite silkiness of her back as we moved effortlessly in the glow of the enchanting harbor lights.

We slowly danced out to the circular balcony that surrounded the casino and commanded the most magnificent, unencumbered view of the harbor on the island. Once outside, she again took my hand, and we casually strolled around the balcony, away from the harbor to an area of little light, shielded from the maddening crowd within. We embraced and passionately kissed with probing tongues and groping caresses. I moved from her sumptuous lips down her neck, softly kissing her shoulder and nuzzling the strap out of the way, allowing it to slip down her arm. I continued to gently kiss her chest then slowly made my way down to her unyielding breast. I caressed one smooth breast with my hand, while softly kissing the other, gently seizing the erect nipple between my lips. My other hand placidly explored the moist warmth between her tender thighs.

Yes, I admit that I am an unrepentant, unadulterated cad. No doubt about it. My threshold of temptation has always been pubescently obscure, and the exhilaration of purloined forbidden fruit always entices me as an immoral conquest. It is always more exciting to surreptitiously gain the favors of another man's lover, especially when the seductive paramour's significant other is the likes of the womanizing, god-like creature Nicky Fallon. It is quite an ego boost and had a robust effect upon Thor the Barbarian.

Our torrid grope fest continued until finally, during a brief respite, we imagined that we had expended about as much time and energy as we dared, lest we run the risk of discovery. We reshuffled our attire, fussed with our hair, and wiped lipstick off each other's assorted appendages. We performed a cursory inspection to prevent any embarrassment upon our return to bright lights and prying eyes.

Confident that all was in order, we held hands and continued our casual stroll around the promenade, as if the ten-minute disappearance was simply a beguiling warp of time, a bubbly induced lapse of awareness.

We reentered the casino from the front of the building, and of course, it seemed as though all eyes were keenly upon us. It was only my imagination perhaps, except for Nicky Fallon and Mrs. Rigney, who both noted our arrival upon our return. She wore a wicked, knowing little smile; he definitely did not.

Before we parted company and went our separate ways, she asked if we might have lunch together one of these afternoons. The prospect of consummating the evening's foreplay was exhilarating. I told her tomorrow was impossible, but that I had no particular agenda for the following day. We agreed to a tentative lunch the day after tomorrow, location yet to be decided. With that, we bid each other ado and returned to our respective partners.

As I moved toward where Mrs. Rigney was socially ensconced, she excused herself from the adoring multitude and joined me at the bar.

"Well," she asked knowingly, "did you enjoy the tour under the evening stars?"

"Yes," I said. "I needed a breath of fresh air."

She made a mocking sniff of the air and said playfully, "Hmmm, the scent of lilacs in the air."

I excused myself and went to wash up before she did anymore sniffing around.

Upon my exit from the washroom, I ran into Harry Peters. He apparently was satisfied with the working arrangements, and we agreed to meet at our designated office space tomorrow morning at nine.

Before rejoining Mrs. Rigney, I called the mansion from a phone near the restrooms. Spaulding assured me that everything was in order. Mr. Rigney had retired for the evening, as had Consuela, the housekeeper, and cook. Manuel was monitoring the front gates and periodically checking the grounds as I had instructed. Satisfied that all was as it should be, I informed Spaulding that we would probably return shortly and bid him a good evening.

I rejoined Mrs. Rigney at the bar, where she asked if I would like to accompany her to a local bistro for a nightcap. I told her I would like nothing better than to join her where I could loosen my tie and let my hair down. We gathered our belongings, bid farewell to the maddening crowd, and made our way outside for a refreshing stroll under the soft moonlight amid twinkling stars and a balmy evening breeze.

It was a glorious evening as we walked along the boardwalk at the water's edge. Lights danced upon the water, and the night was filled with the sounds of festive music and the laughter of happy island revelers. It felt wonderful walking beside her as she held close to my arm. Perhaps it was the enchanting evening, or maybe it was the champagne; either way, I knew it was a bad idea, but I couldn't help myself. I took her in my arms and kissed her passionately. She accepted softly and tenderly.

"I knew it," she said playfully. "Dugan, you're a hopeless romantic."

Chapter 5

After Hours

We walked along the boardwalk to the south end of town. We turned away from the harbor and walked about half a block up a side street, following the boisterous singing and laughter until we finally arrived at the Marlin Club.

The Marlin Club was a small, dimly lit pub frequented by local fishermen, longshoremen, divers, seafarers, adventurers, and assorted barnacle scrapers. Naturally, the motif was nautical décor with the accompanying chum bucket ambient aroma. It was dark and smoky and filled with loud, turbulent, deep-water scoundrels and rogues, a distinct contrast to the elegant sublimity of the casino. Our formal eveningwear made us stick out like virgin cousins at an Appalachian lap dance.

Conspicuous attire aside, it made little difference. Immediately upon our arrival, all the scalawags greeted Mrs. Rigney on a first-name basis and invited her to join them in drunken merriment. As we made our way along the bar, she welcomed each happy character she encountered. It was like a class reunion of the peg-leg fraternity. She apparently was acquainted with every scurvied, rum-suckin' rascal on the Barbary Coast.

We navigated to a safe mooring at the end of the bar, across from a small bandstand in the corner. The ensuing entertainment upon our arrival was none other than the intrepid Captain Wally. He merrily played his squeezebox concertina and danced a lively sea ditty in the middle of a throng of rapscallions who were clapping and dancing. It was a lively little tavern, and all those aboard were having a good time.

The proprietor was a stout, weathered salt of a gal named Sally. She had flaxen hair that resembled dried straw, and her tanned skin was wrinkled and drawn. The deep lines in her face were well earned; they framed a constant smile and happy, twinkling eyes. She was a "high-miler," but obviously had a rousing good time getting there. Mrs. Rigney told me, between sips from her frothy tankard of ale, that Sally's husband had abandoned her during a vacation to the island many years ago. Penniless, but undaunted, she worked hard and made a good life for herself in her adopted seafaring community. She was a warm-hearted, salt-of-the-earth, fun-loving lady, and everybody adored her.

Captain Wally finished his animated performance and wheezed back to the bar, gladly accepting the cool tankard that Sally had set out next to us.

"Well, polliwog, I see you've wasted no time at all in takin' up with the most beautiful angel on the island," said the old captain after a breathless gulp of ale.

"I see I'm not the only one who calls you angel," I said.

"Yes, I was going to ask you about that," she replied.

"You must be an angel," I said. "Only a guardian angel could have gotten us out of a jam like you did today."

"You got that right, polliwog," said the captain. "And you know, she not only looks like an angel, she sings like one, too. She has a voice that will melt your heart, this one does."

"Come on, angel," he coaxed, "sing one for the boys."

Captain Wally went and fetched Sampson, a black piano player with a wide smile and happy-go-lucky personality. Sampson sat at the piano and began playing a soulful blues riff. She made her way to the stage and with that cattish glance from under long delicious lashes, began. Her voice was deep and smoky. She sang a sad, "lost my man" blues ballad by Billie Holiday. It was so quiet in the pub you could hear a pin drop. Before she was through, every buccaneer in the place had tears in his eyes and wanted to call his momma. She was gorgeous and sexy and knew how to deliver a tune. I could see how she had once made a great living at this; she was dynamite.

After the tear-jerking, heart-wrenching ballad, Sampson broke into an upbeat toe-tapper that everyone recognized and immediately began clapping along to and whooping it up. She smiled wickedly and began her party favorite with a line something like, "He likes to nibble on my cupcakes." Each line was punctuated by uproarious laughter and degenerated into a tawdry ditty of sexual innuendo that had the assembled miscreants rolling on the floor with delight. She was a fun girl and knew how to work a party. She amazed me; not only could she schmooze with the high-falutin' social crowd, but she was the life of the party among the hard-livin' working stiffs. I saw why everyone loved her.

She finished with a couple more raunchy party songs, punctuated with animated butt-shakes and open-armed titty-wiggles that set the place afire. She was the life of the party and left the stage with everyone begging for more. She was a great girl and a real trooper. I was falling in love.

It was an old habit of mine to sit with my back to the wall, facing the room and the door. That way I could observe all that occurred in the joint and be aware of any new arrivals. It was no different in the casino or the Marlin Club. The practice had served me well on numerous occasions. I think it may have been a lesson I learned as a kid reading dime store western novels. No gunslinger worth his salt would ever be caught dead sitting with his back to the door.

As Mrs. Rigney made her way back to the bar stool next to me, I looked past her and noticed the fat man had been lingering in the shadows by the door, sans the Chinese gargantuan. He ambled over to where we sat, seemingly enjoying the excitement of this ruffians' lair, judging by the wide grin on his round, ruddy face. He eventually arrived at our location, removed his bowler, and with wide grin still firmly affixed, introduced himself.

"Madam," he began, "I simply had to compliment you on your unique and stimulating talent. Very entertaining, very entertaining, indeed! Allow me to introduce myself. I am Sir Arthur Sydney at your service."

"Happy to make your acquaintance, Sir Arthur," she replied. "May I introduce my friend, Mr. Dugan?"

"Pleased to meet you, Mr. Dugan," he said as we shook hands. "Very pleased, indeed. Perhaps I could invite you to join me for refreshments." He motioned to a table in the back, through beaded curtains. We agreed, and the three of us adjourned to the table in the quiet alcove. It was getting late in the evening, so I opted for java, and Mrs. Rigney followed suite. The fat man ordered cognac.

"So, Sir Arthur," I began, half jesting. "You're a nobleman to king and country?"

"Aahh!" He laughed heartily. "If only it were so," he replied. "Although I have indeed dutifully served the throne discreetly on a number of occasions, to be totally honest, the title is an acquired appellation."

I turned to Mrs. Rigney with a puzzled look.

"What Sir Arthur is so eloquently, yet elusively, stating," she said, "is that he bought it."

"Aaahh!" he laughed again. "Exactly right you are, my dear. Indeed. Bought and paid for. Signed, sealed, and delivered, as they say."

The fat man took a long, loving pull from his cognac, leaned back in his chair, which strained and creaked under his opulent girth, and laughed aloud again. He certainly seemed to be enjoying himself.

"The truth of the matter is," he continued, "that a certain nobleman, who shall remain anonymous, owed a considerable gambling debt to yours truly. His only means of retribution was to relinquish his title, which of course, I graciously, though reluctantly, accepted. Realistically, the title is worth 'diddley,' as I believe you Americans phrase it. However, it does open a few doors that would not ordinarily be available to me. A minor convenience that allows me an introduction or appointment here or there. Nothing more than that, I'm afraid. The title does sound rather impressive over the phone; therefore, it usually gets me moved to the top of the list for dinner reservations. Aahh!" He laughed out loud again. "And as you can readily see, that is an advantage I tend to utilize, and perhaps flaunt, on a regular basis." He playfully patted his preponderance.

"If you don't mind my asking," I interjected, "what line of work are you in?"

"Ah, yes," he exclaimed, "cut to the chase—no beating around the bush. I must admit, Mr. Dugan, I love that uniquely American characteristic. Likewise, I'm enthralled with phrases that describe those peculiar behaviors. The really—oh, what is that phrase I'm looking for?"

"Hit the nail on the head?" I asked.

"Yes, exactly," he responded. "Hit the nail on the head. I, sir, am what might be described, in less sophisticated circles, as a cultural mercenary. Or perhaps, to be less subversive, an intellectual soldier of fortune."

Again, I looked quizzically to Mrs. Rigney. She smiled, shrugged her shoulders, and said, "Artisan bounty hunter. High-priced salvage consultant."

"Right you are again, my dear," he laughed. "Give the lovely lady a kewpie doll."

The fat man ordered another cognac and lit, with great ceremony, a big ugly Cuban cigar. He, of course, asked the lady's permission before doing so. His cognac arrived and he leaned precariously back in his seriously inadequate chair.

"As you no doubt are aware," he began, "there are, at any given time, but especially now after the unfortunate recent world conflagration, a great many treasures, artifacts, statuary, and other works of art, paintings, jewelry, gem stones, and antiquities of all sorts scattered about the globe. One could find such things in any number of auctions, bazaars, estates, or cubbyhole one might imagine. I possess a certain talent for locating such lost treasure and making them available to collectors or the highest bidders. Aaahh, yes, indeed," he continued. "Of course, on occasion, I have a sponsor who requests a particular item. In those instances, I am retained indefinitely, and my expenses are reimbursed. I prefer, however, to come into the possession of a sought-after item of great value, by whatever means, and sell it outright on the open market. The risk is greater, but so are the rewards. At any rate, it affords me the lifestyle to which I have become thoroughly accustomed, and I enjoy traveling the world and partaking in its decadent pleasures. Ahh, yes, indeed I do."

"I assume, then," asked Mrs. Rigney, "that you'll be attending the art auction tomorrow night, Sir Arthur?"

"Oh, yes, indeed," he responded. "You never can tell what you might find at such functions. I'm looking forward to the experience with great anticipation. Indeed I am."

At that moment, the small alcove darkened. A huge figure stood menacingly in the doorway, blocking the light from the main room.

"Ah, yes, my friend—come and sit down," said the fat man. "I'd like to introduce you to my charming guests."

The giant Chinaman I had seen earlier with the fat man at the casino stepped into the room, taking up the remainder of the unoccupied space, and squeezed himself into a stressed chair in the corner.

"Mrs. Rigney, Mr. Dugan, allow me to introduce my associate Phangs Pa."

Phangs Pa—a huge imposing creature, a granite monument wedged into a pinstriped suit. The fu man chu, and the long, straight hair pulled tight into a single pony-tail in the back created the look of a comic book caricature, albeit a really big scary one.

The fat man motioned for Sally, and when she arrived, he ordered a pot of tea for his large, non-imbibing friend.

"So, Mr. Dugan," the fat man began, "if I may inquire, what brings you to this enchanting little island? Are you an art connoisseur, perhaps?"

"No, nothing as flamboyant as that, I'm afraid," I responded. "I'm just here to enjoy the sights and assist with a bookkeeping audit."

"You'll excuse me for saying so, my friend," the fat man interrupted. "But you don't appear the accountant type. No, I would say you are more worldly than your average accountant. Perhaps a little too rough around the edges for a bookkeeper. A little too scarred, a little too tough for either profession. My guess would be something a bit more sinister, more intriguing. I believe you're in a profession that would require a certain amount of aggression and a disproportionate amount of self-confidence and rugged individuality. No, my friend," he concluded, "a bookkeeper or accountant? I think not. No indeed, my friend."

The fat man leaned back in his chair once more, sipping from his snifter, and drawing from his cigar. He had a twinkle in his eye and the look of a mischievous adolescent enjoying the machinations of a juvenile mind game. He raised his eyebrows in expectant anticipation of my response. I looked over at the oversized Neanderthal who sat calmly sipping his tea with no discernible outward expression. The Chinese Bigfoot was rather comical, sipping from what looked like a demitasse cup held in his ham hock-sized hand and Polish sausage fingers.

"How absolutely correct, my obese friend," I finally retorted. "How very acute. Keenly perceptive of you. Very astute. Very astute, indeed."

"Come, come, my friend," said the fat man, leaning forward. "Please do not take offense to my observations. After all, I take a certain amount of pride in my ability to deduce a person's proclivities and motivations. I enjoy discerning the professions of interesting and intriguing individuals. And you, my friend, are a very interesting individual, very interesting indeed. You are the quintessential American—the self-reliant spirit of individuality, the unique American characteristic that sets you Yanks apart from the rest of the downtrodden, ho-hum world."

The fat man had worked himself into whirlwind buzz of excitement this time.

"You, my friend," he continued, "are the embodiment of that undaunted, pioneering pugnaciousness that freed the spiritually oppressed and opened the vast wilderness for the adventurous. You, my friend, are the hired gunslinger so exquisitely romanticized in your dime store novels and Wild West movies."

With that, the fat man leaned far back in his quivering chair, raised his eyebrows and his arms, palms out, as if receiving atonement. He smiled broadly then laughed aloud. He was having a wonderful time, obviously overjoyed with himself.

"That's it!" he exclaimed. "I've guessed it, haven't I, Mr. Dugan? You're here to save the damsel in distress and make right the wrongs. Why, ma'am," he mimicked in his best tobacco-chewin' drawl, "he's fixin' to come down yonder and clean up this here town. Make it a safe place for ya'll God-fearin' folks." He laughed with delight, and even the Mongolian monster attempted a slight resemblance to a smile. "That's it, isn't it, my friend?" chortled the obese one. "I've hit the proverbial nail on the head, haven't I, my iconoclastic compatriot?"

I recognized "Artie" to be the grown-up incarnation of the fat-boy schoolyard bully. They were always too big and fat for anyone to beat up, and if they got involved in an altercation, they put their opponent in a headlock, face jammed mercilessly into a fat, sweaty armpit until the lunch money was relinquished. You know of whom I speak—there's one in every schoolyard. His name is Toby, Stanley, or Junior—the Marquis de Sade reincarnated into a Baby Huey body.

The fat man, having celebrated the verbal joust, now prepared to retire for the evening. He gathered his bowler and cane, wished the lady a pleasant evening, tipped his hat in my direction with a slight bow, then squeezed his abundant circumference through the beaded doorway. His immense cohort followed with a curt bow, and they disappeared into the smoky interior of the Marlin Club and out onto the misty streets of Avalon.

It had been a long day, and I sensed that Mrs. Rigney was as tired as I was. We paid our tab and made our way outside to hail a cab for the ride back to the estate. We arrived at the front gate and our headlights illuminated an ever-vigilant Manuel, still manning the gates. He opened the gate, and as we entered, I asked the driver to stop for a moment. I rolled down the window and asked Manuel if there were any visitors while we were gone. He assured me that there had been no visitors and the policia was still at his post across the street. I thanked him for his help and instructed him to lock the gates after the cab left the estate and turn in for the night. The cab driver deposited us at the front door of the mansion, where Spaulding was waiting. After I said goodnight to Mrs. Rigney and she had gone inside, Spaulding informed me that all was well and the evening had passed with nothing unusual occurring. I thanked Spaulding for his diligence and said goodnight. I walked the short distance across the courtyard to the guesthouse. I barely removed my dinner jacket before collapsing across the big, soft bed and falling into an exhausted sleep.

Chapter 6

The Orientation

Late in the afternoon of a stand-down (non-flying day) for a few of us, we set up a makeshift table in our quarters and indulged in a little low-stakes poker game. As I recall, that was the first and last game of poker I got involved in while flying combat over the Japanese empire.

It was a dull, quiet game. We were just wasting time until our next mission. It was relaxing—a little unusual for me, as I had maintained a full, sometimes hectic schedule to avoid thinking too much about where I was and what I was doing.

It was getting dark and onto chow time, when one of the new additions to the bomb group barged up to the doorway in full flight gear. He was a large, rawboned, blond-headed, two hundred-pound kid—probably in his early twenties—with blood in his eye.

New arrivals to the South Pacific were easily spotted. Replacement crews, "gravel agitators" (non-flying personnel—i.e.: ground crews, engineers, dishwashers), "Shanker mechanics" (MDs), etc. For the first few days or weeks, depending on the guy or gal, they were drenched in perspiration day and night from the nearly one hundred-degree temperatures and high humidity. After a while, everyone adjusted to it and only popped a sweat with exertion.

Anyway, I had my back to the wall and looked to my right at the doorway when the commotion started. This young buck looked me right in the eye and shouted, "I'm going on a mission tonight, and if you come in at two o'clock in the morning and wake me up, banging into everything like you did last night, I'm gonna have a piece a' your ass!"

I calmly and quietly informed the irate young guy that he was mistaken. The previous night, I had been in the sack and sound asleep well before two o'clock, so I couldn't have been the guy that disturbed him.

We were all taken aback a little at the gall of this "Johnny come lately," who couldn't have been on the island but a day or two, throwing his weight around like some long-time VIP with a gnat in his britches. He just wouldn't stop or listen to reason. He raved about what he was going to do. He was going to rip the door off and tear me a new ass, and on and on.

Well, I tired of the raging diatribe after a bit and drew my 45-caliber, pointed it right between his eyes, and informed the young goat that should the door to my room open for any reason in the middle of the night, this was what he would be welcomed with. "Get the hell out of here now, and go take your cherry ride."

His eyes flew open, showing an unusual amount of white, and as in the old western movies, disappeared into the sunset – fast. As fate would have it, this was the kid's orientation flight with the commanding officer. The take-off into the coal-black night and the climb-out was pretty much all instruments; there were little or no visual references. It was solid black, nothing beyond the cockpit. For some reason, a malfunction, incorrect calibration, or whatever—we'll never know—the artificial horizon indicated a normal rate of climb and steadily increasing air speed.

Instead, at full power, the plane mushed, nose-up, into the short over-run area between the end of the eighty-five hundred foot runway and the sea at something over one hundred thirty-five miles per hour. On impact, the fully loaded fuel tanks ruptured, and that beautiful B-29 and its crew of eleven highly trained officers and enlisted men exploded in a fiery holocaust and disappeared into the Pacific Ocean.

I sat bolt upright in the bed, a scream on my lips, in a pool of cold, clammy perspiration. That young, arrogant, outraged pilot of the poker game confrontation, on his very first attempt to put himself "in harm's way," had failed. He perished; he had paid the ultimate price.

I've pondered, many times over the years, if in any way I had contributed to that dreadfully tragic night. But I've long since chalked it up to the fickle finger of fate or the winds of war. Otherwise, how could some of us challenge the inevitable, thumb our noses at the odds dozens of times, rack up hundreds of combat hours, and come through it all without a scratch? Others stick their necks out one time and get the big scythe from the grim reaper in a terrible way. It really makes no sense at all—unless it's pre-ordained. If nothing more, it lends food for thought, lots of thought. There has to be a reason, especially regarding the very young.

I was jarred out of my maudlin, philosophical sojourn into the past by a persistent rapping on the door. It took a few moments for me to clear my head and figure out what year it was. I glanced at the clock on the nightstand next to the bed. The clock read eight; I reasoned AM.

The rapping continued until, in a gruff, foggy tone, I asked who was there. It was Spaulding, reminding curtly that I was due at the casino at nine for the accounting audit. I opened the door, and Spaulding entered, carrying a tray containing breakfast. He set the tray on the small table near the window, removed the morning paper from under his arm, and placed it on the table next to the tray.

"Let me be the first to congratulate you on such a judiciously discreet investigation, Mr. Dugan," he said in his condescending tone. "You've made the front page of our little island journal," he continued, unrelenting. "Unfortunately, the grand ball held at the casino grabbed the headline, but you are featured prominently way down here in the corner."

"A smart ass, this early in the morning, Spaulding, is as about as welcome as wet toilet paper," I said.

"Very well, sir. Should you require any further encouragement, feel free to ring the button next the bed. I shall return with your wardrobe after you've showered." With that, he returned to his duties in the main house.

As soon as he left, I scanned the story about our plunge into the Pacific. It was pretty straight forward—a car accident involving a prominent citizen and her companion. Investigation continuing. The remainder of the front page was awash with every trifling detail of the glittering spectacular that was, "The Ball."

Next, I performed a terse perusal of the contents upon the breakfast tray—a small pot of hot coffee, toast with butter and marmalade, a small glass of orange juice, and a piping hot bowl of creamy oatmeal with a sprinkle of cinnamon. The pièce de résistance, however, was the tall, cool, scarlet bloody mary that stood majestically at the head of the tray, shivering in cool condensation. That Spaulding, he was a real pain in the you-know-where, but he was good. He was very good.

I grabbed the phone next to the bed and brought it to the table. I dialed the operator and gave her the number to my office back on the mainland, as they fondly refer to the unseen shore that was a brown grunge on a distant horizon. While I waited for the connection, I began to wolf down the oatmeal and toast. I had made a respectable dent in both and washed it down with a couple of quick gulps of welcome java by the time I got an answer on the other end of the line.

"Good morning, Travis Dugan Private Investigations," came the bright and efficient female voice over the phone.

"Good morning, Precious," I said. "I guess you're the exception to the old 'while the cat's away the mice will play' rule, huh, sweetheart?"

"Well, aloha, lover boy," she said. "How's the vacation going? Have you fallen in love yet?"

"Oh, the natives are very friendly here," I answered. "I've fallen in lust several times already. But none can compare to the passion that burns within me for you, Precious."

"Oh, stick a sock in it, stud," she retorted. "It's much too early in the morning for this. Seriously, Travis, how's it going?"

"It's going smashingly, duck," I said. "So far, I've had a lei-surely cruise across the channel. I've enjoyed exotic sights, courtesy of an enchanting tour guide. I've relaxed with a sunset swim in Lover's Cove, in the company of the aforementioned guide. And I've been chosen the designated sexual interest to the belle of the ball. We spent last evening in delirious obses-sion of dining, drink, and dancing 'til the wee-wee hours of the morning."

"That's my boy," she said. "Now, you will leave one or two of those innocent young native girls unspoiled, won't you, you maniac?" she asked.

"I'll try to pace myself. Precious, I need you to check out a couple of names for me," I said, getting abruptly to business.

"I knew it was too good to be true," she said. "I just knew you weren't going to Catalina for the pure pleasure of it. Damn you anyway, butthead." There was a poignant pause. "Okay, Sherlock, lay them on me," she finally said reluctantly.

I leaned back in my chair and sipped my bloody mary. "The first one is Chief Inspector Fontaine LaFarge. Thirty-five to forty, approximately six foot, Caucasian, black and brown. No scars, speaks with an accent, not necessarily French. That's about all I have on him right now, though I have a meeting with him this morning. I might find out something more, maybe not. The next one," I continued, "is Nicky Fallon. Twenty-five to thirty, six foot, Caucasian, maybe Italian. Black and brown, no scars, no accent. Nicky is a pretty boy, real lady-killer. Articu-late, seems well educated, might check the eastern universities; he attended college somewhere. The last one is Sir Arthur Sid-ney. Sixty to sixty-five, six foot Caucasian, British—no doubt. Bald and blue, and this crumb snatcher enjoys his meals; he probably runs around three hundred pounds. Says he's some kind of art dealer. I suspect more of a thief or swindler. You got all that, Precious?"

"Sounds like an interesting crowd you're associating with," she said. "What's the scam?"

"Right now, it's still a missing person case," I said. "But there's no telling what this thing could turn into. I'm the new kid on the block, and everybody seems to be a few steps ahead. Right now, I'm playing catch up."

"Well, I'll see what I can find out about these playmates of yours," she said. "How do I get in touch with you?"

"I'll get in touch with you," I said. "I'll call you tomorrow morning. If it's urgent, you can leave word at the Rigney Estate, and I'll get back to you. I left the number on my desk."

"Okay, Travis, take care, and remember—pace yourself," she said with a mischievous laugh.

"Oh, one more thing, doll," I said. "I need the three Musketeers over here to secure the Rigney Estate. How soon can you round them up and get them over here?"

"I'll have them there by this afternoon," she said.

"Okay, Precious; I'll call you tomorrow morning then. Thanks."

I hung up the phone then finished the last morsels left on my breakfast tray. I had to smile; Precious was a great gal, and I don't know how I would get along without her. She was an attractive blond in her late thirties, but looked ten years younger. I'd seen pictures of her in a bathing suit on the beach. In her prime, she was a real knockout. She was a sharp girl and knew her way around. Precious Goodlay had connections for which any self-respecting PI would kill. All her male relatives were members of a police agency of some kind. Her father was in the FBI and now owned his own security agency with contacts in the defense industry. One of her uncles was with Scotland Yard and another with Interpol. If that weren't enough, she had a brother with LAPD homicide, and another was a San Francisco vice detective. Previous Goodlay was worth her weight in gold, and that was just about what I paid her.

She lost her husband Gunnar several years ago. He was an LA beat cop. He was killed when he inadvertently came upon a bank holdup in progress. LA is the bank heist capital of the world. There is a bank of one kind or another in every neighborhood, on every corner. All neighborhoods in the basin sit adjacent to a freeway. The combination makes for fair odds, even for the most clumsy and inept of bank robbers.

I quickly showered, shaved, and picked over the remnants of what had been breakfast. Spaulding arrived with my recycled clothing, all neatly pressed. My hat was re-blocked, and my shoes were shined to a dazzling gloss. Even my standard issue PI trench coat looked new. I dressed and splashed on some frou-frou water, strapped on the old "persuader," hat, and coat and was out the door. It was an overcast morning, but I figured that's the way many mornings started here. I was confident the pall would burn off before long. I decided to check everyone's schedules before I left the estate. I crossed to the main house and knocked on the door. Spaulding answered and followed me into the kitchen, where I found Consuela, the cook, and Manuel, her husband and groundskeeper, finishing their breakfast.

I inquired about everyone's agenda and was assured that all would be on the premises all day. Spaulding informed me that Mrs. Rigney would be attending a public viewing of the items to be auctioned this evening at the museum located in the basement of the casino. The viewing began at one PM; Spaulding anticipated her departure from the estate at around twelve-thirty. I told him I would bring a cab around and escort Mrs. Rigney to the event. I also informed the staff that a security team would be arriving this afternoon and asked that they cooperate as much as possible. I assured them that the security was for the well-being of all and that the team members were professionals and tried to be as nonintrusive as possible. I suggested they be quartered in the guesthouse that I had occupied last night, and any preparations they deemed necessary to accommodate them, I would leave in their capable hands.

I felt confident that I had touched all bases, so I prepared to take my leave. Seeing as how it was all downhill to town, I decided to walk the distance, and work off last night's food and drink extravagance.

Before I could get out the door, Manuel called me aside and asked if he might accompany me down to the front gates. He had something he wanted to show me. He seemed quite concerned, so we hustled down the driveway to the heavy iron gates at the entrance. Just before we got to the gates, we turned to the left and crossed the lawn paralleling the indigenous stone wall that surrounded the estate. When we reached the corner where the walls joined, Manuel motioned me over to the well-cultivated flowerbed that ran along the inside of the walls. He bent down and brushed aside the leaves of a small shrub, and there in the soil was a deep footprint. This wasn't just any footprint; this thing had to be size thirteen, or better. A Sasquatch could have left this footprint. There was something else peculiar about the print. Whatever made the impression appeared to have webbed toes. I looked, puzzled, over to Manuel.

He raised his eyebrows and simply said, "Cooley slippers."

Yes, he was right. I had spent enough time in LA's Chinatown to recognize the print that would be left by what resembled a mitten for your foot. The Chinese wore them like socks. The space sown into the slippers between the big toe and the next was where the thongs of their sandals were designed to fit.

"Very good, Manuel," I said. "Do you know anybody on the island that would have a foot this big?" I asked.

"No, Señor Dugan," he responded. "Muy grande, no?"

"Muy grande, yes," I said. "The person who made this print would be a giant."

I asked Manuel to go the house after I left and ask Spaulding and Consuela to inspect the inside of the house for signs of entry then to go over the remainder of the grounds carefully and look for other prints or indications that someone who did not belong had been on the estate.

Before we parted, Manuel pointed out the broken tree branch that was conspicuously out of place on the other side of the wall, outside the estate. "Like the Indians, they use the branch to sweep away their footprints," he said.

I was impressed. Manuel certainly knew what was what in and around the grounds. I complimented him on his keen observations and asked that he try to preserve the print he had discovered as best he could. I told him I had an appointment with the chief inspector this morning and would report the intrusion. I patted Manuel on the back, bid him a "Buenos dias," and was off toward the front gates and on the road headed for town.

True to his word, Inspector LaFarge still had a man posted outside the estate in a black and white. As I strolled past, briskly moving down the hill, the alert officer waved and said good morning. I wondered if he was as congenial last night when the intruder scaled the wall not fifty yards away.

I arrived in town a short time later, feeling refreshed and invigorated. The morning mist was already starting to clear, and the town was bustling with fishermen haggling with restaurateurs over the price of the morning's catch and shopkeepers preparing for the day's first onslaught of tourists arriving on the nine o'clock steamer.

I breezed through town by the harbor, peering down into the water at the bright garibaldi that swam near the shore. I arrived at the casino and climbed the ramp that went up the outside of the building to the employees' entrance. Inside were a catacomb of office cubicles and a cadre of office personnel busy depositing record books, receipts, bank deposits, etcetera upon the desk occupied by one Harold Peters.

We exchanged greetings while I inventoried the female office staff. *I must remember to compliment the personnel manager.* Before I could grab a cup of coffee, donut, or a secretary, Harry handed me several sheets of paper that appeared to contain items of inventory—furniture, statuary, art works, paintings. The list was endless and varied. Harry informed me that the items on the lists should be found in the attic storage area above the casino and in the basement downstairs next to the museum. He handed me a ring of door keys and dispatched me like a Chinese laundry boy. I didn't particularly appreciate Harry's attitude this morning, but it would be more of a hassle for me to confront him about it than it was just to take my list and ring of keys and blow. Besides, it gave me an excellent excuse to snoop around the place. Ya never know what skeletons you might find in the closets.

I climbed the stairs to the attic and after fumbling with the keys, I finally came up with the one that unlocked the door. Inside was quiet and still, but it was relatively clean, though dusty, and plenty of light came from the skylights high overhead. I took a quick look around and recognized several of the items on my inventory sheet. I went around and opened a few crates, shuffled through a couple drawers, and lifted a few dust covers. Seeing as how I didn't find anything glaringly out of the ordinary, and seeing as how I didn't particularly feel like digging through a bunch of musty furniture and boxes of old crap, I decided that I would find out what treasures I might find in the basement. I locked the attic door behind me and made my way down a labyrinth of interior stairwells to the basement.

The basement was similar in shape to the attic, and for that matter, the rest of the casino, in that it was circular and had plenty of windows, allowing ample light. The area was filled with ornate, antique furniture of all descriptions— armoires, roll-top desks, tiger-grain oak upright pianos, couches, chairs, slot machines, roulette tables, and all types of statuary and paintings. The place was filled to the gunnels with dust-covered treasures that ranged from priceless antiquities to pure crapola.

Again, I spent considerable time digging through drawers, cabinets, and boxes. There seemed to be a lot more documents, papers, and ledgers here than in the attic. Neither area had had much traffic through them in the recent past. They had been virtually untouched and intact for some time. A fine dust had settled on everything exposed, and when items were moved, a clean surface was revealed beneath. It also was clear that there were many more items here than were listed on the inventory sheets I possessed.

The morning mist had cleared to reveal a bright, sparkling blue sky, which could be seen through the high windows of my dungeon. Just the thought of being shackled to laborious toil for days was particularly depressing. I wondered what Harry the toad boy had in mind when he assigned me this dust-choking sentence. Did he want me out of the way? Did he want all those leggy secretaries searching through bottom drawer filing cabinets to himself? Did he figure he would give me all the dirty work? The answer was, of course, "yes," on all counts.

I rationalized that I could not expend the proper amount of time due this assignment, this afternoon, because of my appointment with the "Good Inspector Frenchy LaFarge." I also was to escort Mrs. Rigney to the public art exhibition at the museum this afternoon. I closed the basement door, locked it, dropped the ring of keys into my coat pocket, and made a surreptitious escape to the outside world, clinging to the walls like a convict who had just dropped off the end of a knotted sheet. It was a bright blue day, and the mist far in the distance obscured the horizon where sea and sky met.

I strolled along the harbor and noticed that several of the boats competing in the regatta at the end of the week had already arrived. Efficient young crews checked rigging in preparation for the morning's sea trials. As I passed the museum entrance across the promenade from the harbor, I noticed the addition of uniformed guards posted on either side of the double glass doors. Through the doors, within the museum itself, the excited hubbub of the afternoon's auction preparations were evident—much scurrying about, hands on hips, pointing, beefy men humping large, apparently heavy statuary to and fro.

I continued past the yacht club and walked out to the end of the steamer pier. The big white steamer lay nestled in calm repose, having spewed happy, bouncy morning arrivals, and preparing for the morning's first return trip to the mainland. I leaned on the pier rail and gazed, unfocused, at the blue-gray canvas, dashed boldly with bright splashes of white and red. All fluttering and windswept, sun-bleached and salt water tans. I wondered how amiable the good inspector was apt to be this morning in the harsh light of day.

So far, the leads I'd developed in the case of one Johnny Rigney had for the most part gotten me zip, zilch, nada, nyet—the big goose egg. No motive and no suspects, other than the obvious—the immediate family and staff, but those possibilities seemed remote at best. All the family members had plenty of money, more than they could spend in a lifetime. And people all over the world continued to eat those candy bars, so it seemed a reasonable assumption that family members would continue to amass tremendous wealth.

The servant staff had been with the family for years and seemed devoted and loyal. They all seemed satisfied with their stations in life, perhaps even grateful and appreciative for the family's concern for their well-being, their graciousness, and generosity. I knew I would have to dig deeper into the relationships within the family and household staff, but at this point, nothing seemed glaringly out of the ordinary. Money did not seem a likely motive. And from what I'd seen so far, except for the two Rigney women, passion would not be a likely crime for which the staff could be accused. Suspects outside the family? Well, let's see what Precious came up with. The three names I gave her were a starting point. We'd proceed from there. I checked my watch. The inspector would be waiting.

I walked back along the pier and tried to imagine how today's interrogation might progress. As with most police officials, who view me and my ilk as flies in the ointment, I expected him to be rude and annoyed at having to deal with me. None of them ever appreciated having private investigators mucking about, competing with them for evidence and witness statements during the course of an on-going investigation. The police figure we're untrained, unsupervised clods mucking around in their official business. They get particularly annoyed if one of us happens to crack a case right under their noses. They get down right ugly. They also are extremely piqued that, often, we don't necessarily abide strictly by the rules regarding the accumulation of information, as they are theoretically required to do.

Although my official reason for being here was the casino audit, it was a flimsy cover, and I'm sure the good inspector was suspicious of my true intentions. Inspector LaFarge seemed extremely authoritarian. He would resist any usurpation of his power or trespassing upon his territory.

Something else to consider was the possibility that the police had fished the body of the sedan driver out of the cove and discovered four bullet holes in it. That possibility could put me in a tight spot, even though it was self-defense, and I had an impeccable witness. It would still give LaFarge a good excuse to squeeze me like a ripe fruit.

Then there was the question of the sedan driver's intended victim. Who was he trying to kill, and why? And what did the attempt on our lives have to do with the disappearance of Johnny Rigney?

I walked back to the boardwalk, then on up the street to the small, quaint Victorian two-story that housed police headquarters. I checked in with the desk sergeant and was escorted to Chief Inspector LaFarge's office. It was an antiseptic, spit and polish environment void of personal mementos or family photos.

Inspector LaFarge sat behind his desk, viewing the contents of an open file. He motioned me to a chair across the desk from him and quietly continued to inspect the file. He finally closed the file, looked up, and clasped his hands on top of his desk. "Good morning, Mr. Dugan," he began. "I appreciate your punctuality. Of course, you realize that I must have your statement regarding yesterday's mishap for the official report. Suppose you tell me in your own words what occurred."

I related the story of yesterday's excitement, leaving out only the four shots through the sedan windshield. LaFarge starred at me intently throughout the entire dissertation and did not attempt to interrupt. When I finished, the inspector began to ask the obvious questions: Did I have any enemies that would make an attempt on my life? Did I get a look at the driver of the sedan? Would my presence on the island or my reasons for being here be cause for alarm from anyone? All predictable questions and, as I told the good inspector, questions I had asked myself. The only question I could answer with any conviction was the one regarding the identity of the sedan driver. I never got a good look at him; therefore, I could not identify him. It seemed an opportune point upon which to ask a few questions of my own.

I began by stating the possibility that the would-be assassin was not after me, but Mrs. Rigney. A possibility the inspector had also considered, thus the black and white parked outside the estate. I thanked him for his prudence, and he nodded. I said if I knew the identity of the driver, it might shed some light on the motive. LaFarge opened the file he had been perusing upon my arrival and began divulging the contents with little apparent hesitation or editing.

"The sedan had been off-loaded onto the freight tarmac only that morning, shipped from the mainland, destined for the Catalina Cab Company, to be added to their fleet of limousines. Apparently, it was especially important for the influx of VIPs ashore for this week's cultural events. Unfortunately," he continued, "what remains there might have been of the driver were thrown into the cove during the crash and carried away and devoured by sharks. We've checked missing persons, of course, but came up with nothing."

There were more pages in the file, but the inspector didn't continue. I figured I'd move the conversation along, perhaps score a few brownie points by reporting the intrusion at the Rigney Estate last night. Inspector LaFarge seemed particularly surprised and began taking notes. I stated the facts, leaving out the details of the peculiar footprint in the soil. I further informed the inspector that Spaulding and the housekeeper were conducting a thorough search of the residence for signs of forced entry or burglary. I promised the inspector that if any information turned up, he would be the first to know.

At this point, not having encountered much resistance from the vigilant inspector thus far, I decided to press for information. "I understand there is a pending missing person's case regarding Mrs. Rigney's husband, Johnny," I dove right in. "Do you think it could have any connection with the attempt on her life yesterday or the intrusion on the estate last night?" I asked, as innocuously as possible.

He stared at me intently for a moment with dark, piercing eyes. "First of all, Mr. Dugan," he began sternly, "it has not been conclusively established that the attempt was on Mrs. Rigney; perhaps you were the intended target. Secondly, I can assure you that Mr. Rigney's case has been thoroughly investigated from every angle. We went so far as to assume that the deck hand, Miguel, could have been the target or the perpetrator of a crime. To this day, there is nothing that makes us suspect that the incident was anything more than a boating accident. And I caution you; I am using 'boating accident' in general terms. We found nothing in the way of debris. They simply sailed out of the harbor on a bright sunny day with calm seas and off the face of the earth."

I pondered what the good inspector had divulged for a few brief moments then forged ahead. "Have there been any similar boat disappearances in recent years?"

The inspector slowly worked his scowl into the semblance of a small smile. He leaned back in his chair and stroked his thin mustache. He seemed amused. "Well, well, my friend!" he finally said. "It seems I have discovered initial indications of the pugnacious, bull dog of a PI that your reputation indicates. You seem more refined, more sophisticated, than the crude brute one would imagine from a preliminary scan of your past."

"That's why I get the big money," I interjected. I should have kept my mouth shut.

He was not amused. "You see," he continued. "We went to the trouble of running a background check on you, my friend. We received mixed reviews from various sources within the LAPD. However, the consensus seems to be that you are tough, tenacious, cunning, and deadly." He paused for reaction. There was none. He leaned forward in his chair and lowered his voice, speaking slowly and with intent. "Mr. Dugan, there seems to be a significant increase in the number of cadavers arriving at the LA County morgue when you are involved in a case. You appear to be a loose cannon, if you will. Let me caution you in no uncertain terms, Mr. Dugan, that I will not tolerate some shoot from the hip, ask questions later cowboy roaming the streets of Avalon. We will be keeping a close eye on you, my friend. I suggest strongly that you keep your weapon and other appendages where they belong."

Now it was my turn to lean back in my chair and smile. That was a very intriguing final comment from the good inspector. Was that jealousy rearing its ugly head? Did he secretly yearn for Mrs. Rigney? Perhaps it was the vivacious Rita Rigney that the inspector was enamored of. I let the comment go without reply or change in demeanor. "Have there been any boat disappearances under similar circumstances in the recent past?"

Constable LaFarge again sat upright in his chair and folded his hands in front of him. "There have indeed been several recent boat disappearances. However, I caution you again. This is not information we care to have broadcast all over the island. We do not wish to drive away the tourists and pampered pleasure-seekers with unsubstantiated rumors and half-baked theories. We do not wish to become known as the Bermuda Triangle of the Pacific. Therefore, I suggest, in the strongest possible terms, that you keep this information to yourself. As you no doubt have become aware, this is a small island, and rumors travel quickly."

"Yes, I believe I've heard that observation before," I said. "And have the other investigations into the boat disappearances resulted in the same conclusions? Or lack thereof?" I asked.

"Don't push your luck, my friend," said the inspector. "But, yes, I'm afraid the investigations have turned up very little. I am concerned, and I assure you that the investigations will continue until we get to the bottom of this."

I hoped no pun was intended. We had come to the end of our conversation, and it was almost time for me to round up a cab, retrieve Lara Rigney, and escort her to the museum. I thanked Chief Inspector LaFarge for his cooperation and concern. As we parted company, I assured him I would check with the staff at the mansion and report back to him if anything out of the ordinary were discovered.

I exited police headquarters and walked the short distance to Crescent Avenue, the main ocean front street that ran the length of downtown, parallel to the boardwalk and harbor. When I reached the corner, I dropped a coin in the pay phone and dialed the estate. I got Spaulding on the line and asked if Mrs. Rigney was ready to go and if they had discovered anything during their search. Spaulding said Mrs. Rigney would be ready when I arrived, and that they had indeed found a possible point of entry for the intruder. Before Spaulding hung up, he informed me that there had been a message from my office advising me that my associates would be arriving on the seaplane tarmac at noon today.

I hung up the phone, stepped out to the curb, and whistled for a taxi. Roscoe, the cabbie that drove Lara and me from the estate last night, pulled to a stop at the curb. Roscoe was a middle-aged black cabbie with a constantly surprised expression and a wide, toothy smile.

"Good afternoon, Mr. Dugan," he said as I got in. Roscoe had a friendly, gravelly voice that made him sound as though he was in a constant state of high anxiety. The voice was a perfect match to his appearance. "Where to, boss?"

I told Roscoe that we were to retrieve some friends of mine at the seaplane tarmac, then head up to Rigney Estate. He engaged the meter, and down the road we went. During the ride, we discussed the influx of tourists and the arrival from all over the world of the "high society set" that occurred this time every year. It apparently was one of the high points of the social season. The island's festivities were at the beginning of the season, and anybody who was somebody felt obliged to attend. It was also a lot of fun, no matter your social status. A trip to paradise.

I asked him specifically about Sir Arthur and his baccarat opponent, the dapper English gentleman. Roscoe told me that he had never seen either of the gentlemen on the island before. He had recognized plenty of arrivals from previous visits, but the two Englishmen and the Chinese gargantuan were on the island for the first time.

We arrived just as the weathered, red, Grumman mono-wing splashed in for a carnival ride landing. After a couple of heart stopping bounces, for the benefit of the excited tourists aboard, she taxied up the ramp to the tarmac. The camera-laden throng of Hawaiian shirted straw hats began to emerge from the plane, their animated conversations a tribute to the pilot's efforts on their behalf. It was an exciting conclusion to an airborne roller-coaster ride, and they were thrilled—a great beginning to an adventure that they'd cherish for the rest of their days.

I noticed that Roscoe tensed when my three associates approached. Perhaps it was the fourth member of the party that made Roscoe uneasy. Bogie was a massive, black Rottweiler/pit bull mix—a taut bag of pumped up muscle wrapped around a steel-coil frame. He was a polished ebony nightmare of gnashing jaws and glistening, great white fangs. Bogie was a snorting, flesh-ripping, bone-crushing, frothing frenzy of snarling viciousness. The dog jumped into the front seat next to Roscoe. He stared at him, six inches from the side of Roscoe's face. The ever-present look of surprise remained frozen upon Roscoe's face, but the wide smile faded fast. Roscoe was terrified of the dog, and the dog knew it. Bogie would never harm Roscoe, but he enjoyed his innocent game of intimidation.

Bogie stared at the side of Roscoe's head as we drove to the estate. I could hear Roscoe saying almost silently, "Good doggy, good doggy," as we proceeded.

I assured Roscoe that the dog would not hurt him and was only playing his favorite canine mind game. Apparently, my assurances of safety did not alleviate Roscoe's apprehension as he began to beg, "Sweet Jesus, don't let that dog bite me."

We arrived at the gates, and Roscoe impatiently waited for Manuel to come and open them. He wasn't about to honk the horn. Not with that dog sitting next to him. Bogie had added a low, guttural growl to his routine. The only thing moving on Roscoe was the beads of perspiration beginning to roll down his temples.

Manuel eventually appeared, and we drove through the estate to the guesthouse. We unloaded the bags and deposited them in the team's temporary quarters with no assistance from Roscoe. He remained frozen in his seat with Bogie keeping him company.

It was a cruel joke to play on Roscoe. Bogie was a real scary dog. Bogie was where the phrase, "Tearing someone a new ass," originated. If you look up "Tearing someone a new ass," in the dictionary, you'll find a picture of Bogie.

Before exiting the cab, Bogie growled menacingly under his breath and leaned closer to the paralyzed Roscoe. Sweat poured off him, his kneecaps quivered. As Roscoe began to visibly quake with fright, Bogie leaned over and gave him a big, sloppy kiss that covered half of Roscoe's face. Roscoe relaxed a little and his wide smile began to reappear on his face. I swear I saw the dog smile, too. He gave Roscoe a quick bark then leaped from the cab.

"That's some dog you got there, boss," Roscoe sighed as he shoved his cap back on his head and wiped his brow.

"That was a mean thing to do to you, Roscoe. I apologize for indulging Bogie's twisted game. He really does enjoy intimidating cab drivers. It's some kind of fetish with him. I know it's sick and perverted to let him continue, but who's got enough cajones to give him any lip? You know what I mean, Roscoe?"

"I'm hip, boss," replied Roscoe. "I imagine the cab rides where you come from are the direct-route variety. I don't imagine they be doin' much sight-seeing when that dog be aboard."

I laughed and patted Roscoe on the shoulder. He was a good guy. I paid the fare and tossed him an extra twenty.

"Call me anytime, boss," Roscoe said with his trademark smile. "But maybe next time the dog can ride in the back, huh, boss?"

I assured Roscoe that I would discuss the possibility with Bogie before our next trip then asked Roscoe to remain until Mrs. Rigney and I were ready to return to town.

While the security team stowed their gear and got a feel for the place, I decided to check with Spaulding and investigate the point of entry they had discovered. Upon entering the main house, Spaulding led me to a sitting room off the foyer. The double French doors had been jimmied, and there was a faint trail of what had been wet prints across the highly polished floor on over to the carpet. The prints were obscure and undefined, but they were the same size as the one Manuel found in the garden.

Consuela entered the room, and I asked if anything was missing. She said she was relatively sure nothing was, but she thought everything had been moved and all the drawers had been searched. She explained that she cleaned this room at least twice a week and always closed the drawers and cabinets completely. When she checked the house as I had instructed, she noticed that all the drawers and doors on the bottom floor of the house were uncharacteristically ajar.

It appeared to Consuela, and Spaulding agreed, that someone had carefully searched the ground floor of the mansion during the night. Consuela assured me that the upstairs rooms remained as they should, but she was obviously shaken at the thought of an intruder skulking about in the darkness.

I felt it was an opportune time to introduce the house staff to the security team, in hopes it might alleviate their fears. I gathered the servant staff and the security team in the driveway courtyard. I introduced everyone and allowed Bogie to get acquainted so he could identify them in the dark, if necessary.

I explained that security would be conducted in three shifts for around the clock protection. There would be two shifts of one man each, and the dog and a handler would man the graveyard, or third shift. I advised the staff that it would not be wise to venture out after ten PM unless absolutely necessary, and if possible to inform security of their intentions beforehand.

I was very confident in the ability of the security team and had used their services many times in the past. They were well trained, intelligent, and professional. It was no coincidence that these hulking young bruisers happened to be nephews of my secretary, Precious Goodlay.

The boys operated a lucrative personal and estate security agency that specialized in the needs of the Hollywood entertainment industry. They provided bodyguard and limousine service for movie people, including security on location shoots. The agency they operated also possessed an enviable portfolio of long-term contracts for twenty-four-hour protection of numerous estates located in such posh neighborhoods as Bellaire, Brentwood, Truesdale, the Hollywood Hills, Topanga Canyon, and Malibu.

They had an impressive catalog of important clients because they were discreet, non-intrusive, and fashionably inconspicuous. Hell, they looked like movie stars themselves. They moved effortlessly amongst the professional and social strata.

Just prior to our adjournment, Mrs. Rigney emerged from the mansion in a breezy yellow and white floral print sundress. I introduced the security staff, including Bogie, who was instantly infatuated with her. He melted like an Eskimo Pie left in the afternoon sun.

With that bit of business taken care of, we dispersed to our individual appointments. Mrs. Rigney and I joined Roscoe, dutifully waiting in his cab. On the ride to town, I asked Mrs. Rigney how the Commodore was feeling. She explained that he had experienced a restless night and was not completely lucid this morning. I asked what was wrong with him.

"Nothing is wrong with him, Dugan," she said. "He's just old. He has his good days and his bad days."

It didn't appear as though she wanted to continue that subject any longer, so I didn't pursue it. We proceeded to town in silence.

Chapter 7

The Museum

Upon our arrival at the museum, we received a catalog containing a picture and description of each item on exhibit and a complimentary glass of champagne. The bright airy space was elegantly decorated with paintings, sculpture, and statuary arranged on the high walls and the dark, highly polished floor. It was an impressive turnout, too. Most of the guests present at the ball last night were here, casually enjoying the enlightened glow emanating from the proceedings this afternoon.

Mrs. Rigney and I leisurely strolled around the various exhibits, engaging in courteous chitchat with the other intellectual gadflies. I took note that our quasi-art entrepreneur, the fat man, Sir Arthur, was in attendance and appeared enthralled with the objects d'art in the display case containing antique coins, jewelry, and gemstones. That particular case also contained smaller examples of gold and silver statuary from the far corners of the globe. I had to be careful, lest I absorb far more cultural sophistication than I cared to.

I also noted that the fat man was attending this afternoon's exhibition without the company of his obsequious associate, the Mongolian Goliath. He, no doubt, was out perfecting his nocturnal creepy-crawly techniques. The thought of that monster on the loose with neither muzzle nor leash was unnerving. I felt the urge to grab a whip and a chair.

Mrs. Rigney and I continued our stroll among the illustrious display until we came upon the dapper British baccarat vaquero admiring a dazzling mosaic done in brilliantly colored tiles.

"That's a stunning piece, isn't it?" she said upon our arrival. He turned to Mrs. Rigney and smiled that debonair, rakish smile, and replied, "Beyond my wildest imagination, I should think."

Sexual innuendo with a foreign accent. How cliché. She was eating it up, too. The hussy.

"Allow me to introduce myself," he said. "My name is Pond, Blaine Pond." He bowed and gently kissed her hand, then continued to hold it. "I represent the East-Asian Trading Company, based in Hong Kong and Singapore. I admit a particular fondness for western art and statuary. I'm especially attracted to free-form nudes."

What a load of manure these continental types hauled around and dispensed upon the naïve American nymphets snared by their gossamer net of European accents and mannerisms. You would think that a dame like Lara Rigney would have heard and seen it all before and be way out ahead of the game. Instead, she was lapping it up like the first feline at the milk dish.

"I'm very pleased to meet you, Mr. Pond," she said with flirtation in her voice and wonderfully seductive eyes. "I'd like you to meet my friend Mr. Dugan." She then took his arm and casually moved him away to another work in tile mosaic. I lingered like a stood-up prom date.

I could still overhear their conversation. They were discussing the texture of the medium and the clarity and brilliance of the color. He seemed particularly impressed with the intricacy of the design and the boldness of the piece when viewed in its entirety. He inquired about the origin of the tiles and was delighted to learn that the Catalina Tile Company produced them here on the island. Mr. Pond then asked if the tiles could be purchased in bulk and shipped overseas. Mrs. Rigney assured him that the tile company produced and shipped many large orders around the world. Catalina tile was featured in numerous government buildings, private museums, and other unique architectural structures throughout the world. She then invited him to join her tomorrow, around midday, for a trip to the foundry where the tiles were produced. She would introduce him to the plant manager, and he could tour the operation and discuss future orders and shipping arrangements. With their appointment confirmed, they clicked their champagne glasses gently and bid each other a good afternoon. They separated with lingering glances. I hate that.

Lara Rigney slowly made her way back to where I casually teetered back and forth, hands clasp behind me, cooling my heels.

"Do you think you should be gallivanting around the island with someone you just met and know nothing about?" I asked shortly, still staring at the tiles on the wall in front of me.

"Well," she said sarcastically. "Are we being overprotective, or are we jealous? Or are we just pouting?"

"I'm just trying to do the job you hired me for, ma'am," I snapped, sorry I said it as soon as it came out.

"Oh, I see—it's ma'am now, is it?" she shot back. "Well, now, maybe you know how it feels to be left standing on the dance floor while the person that brought you plays tongue-tango with your sister-in-law out on the balcony."

I stood there with egg on my face and my mouth hanging open for a few uncomfortable moments, temporarily at a loss for words. I slowly recovered from my stupor and simply and humbly responded with "Touché." There was no defending my unconscionable libido. I apologized for my crude behavior and hoped it would suffice.

"Don't get me wrong," she said coyly. "You can pillage and plunder your way across the entire female population of the island. More power to you. Just be a little more discreet. I have a certain position to uphold. I can't be associating with some snake charmer, if you get my drift. And besides," she said with a wicked little smile. "I felt a twinge of jealousy and neglect." She was good. She was really good.

I put my arm around her waist and pulled her close to me. "If you remember, angel," I whispered. "You were supposed to slap me if I got out of line at the ball. Remember? I guess you've got one coming, kid," I said.

"Oh, goody," she said teasingly. "I'll save them up, and we'll make an afternoon of it." *Now that's a mental picture for you.* I sighed heavily.

Mrs. Rigney and I continued touring the exhibits until we found ourselves in the company of the fat man, Sir Arthur Sidney, still intently studying his catalog and the treasures within the rare coins and jewelry display case.

"Good afternoon, Sir Arthur," said Mrs. Rigney. "I see you've discovered something of interest in the sunken treasures area of our little exhibit."

"Oh, Mrs. Rigney and Mr. Dugan," he said with genuine delight. "A glorious afternoon to you as well, my friends. I trust that you are of good cheer on this lovely day?"

"Yes, the sun is shining, the birds are singing, and all is swell with the world," I replied flippantly. "Have you found something you've been seeking?" I asked, carefully studying his reaction to my only slightly veiled implication to the intrusion of last night.

He was silent for a moment, scrutinizing my demeanor for blatant hostility or obscure expeditionary innuendo. "Ahha!" he finally laughed aloud. "Indeed, I have found many articles of interest. I heartily congratulate you, my dear," he said to Mrs. Rigney. "This is a truly magnificent exhibit. The enchanting diversity and the truly unique and substantive pieces are very impressive. Yes, very impressive, indeed."

"Thank you, very much, Sir Arthur," she replied. "Your praise is a highly respected compliment. However, I can't accept the credit for myself. Our museum curator, Sumner Renton, is entirely responsible for the concept and content of the exhibits. I am merely a member of the board of directors, concerned only with budgetary matters."

"You are a very gracious host, my dear," said Sir Arthur. "And far too modest to accept credit where credit is due for a truly magnificent event. You're sophistication and grandeur is reflected in the picturesque serenity of the island. I salute the splendor of your vision and that of the Rigney family's," he concluded with great majesty.

"There's Sumner, right over there," she said, pointing to a demure, bespectacled gentleman speaking with a small group near the entrance. "Would you like me to introduce you, Sir Arthur?"

"I would indeed, Mrs. Rigney," he replied. "I would be honored."

We casually strolled toward the curator. The group he had been conversing with dispersed upon our arrival.

"Hello, Mrs. Rigney," said the curator with gushing enthusiasm. "You're a picture of springtime. That's a lovely sundress. So bright and breezy."

"Thank you, Sumner," she replied with a wide smile. "You're always such an ego booster. Sumner Renton, I'd like you to meet Sir Arthur Sydney, a renown cultural provocateur," she said with a certain jesting delight.

"Ahha!" laughed Sir Arthur, "such a spirited lass. Always a surprisingly delightful creature, I must say. I'm afraid the beautiful and alluring Mrs. Rigney flatters me with un-deserved mystery and intrigue. I am but a simple man with simple needs. No matter how extravagant they may be. Ahha! Ahha!"

"Sir Arthur, I'm very honored to make your acquaintance," said the merry curator. "I hope you find our little gathering entertaining."

"Oh, I do, sir. I do indeed," began the Fat Man. "I was just complimenting Mrs. Rigney on the impressive and diverse grandeur of the event. I am enjoying the experience immensely. I wish to compliment you as well, Mr. Renton," he continued. "The atmosphere you've created is enchanting—a child-like Peter Pan adventure—yet the scope and importance of the genuinely unique exhibits are on par with those found in the most exalted museums in the civilized world. I heartily congratulate you on your accomplishments, sir. Very impressive. Very impressive indeed, sir."

"Thank you, very much," said the humble curator. "It's gratifying to know that one's endeavors have not gone unappreciated, although it would be remiss of me not to acknowledge the contributions of our prolific benefactor, the late P.K. Rigney. He was quite a remarkable man. I must admit I envy his exploits, both archaeologically and romantically. His reputation for romantic conquests in exotic locales was extraordinary. I'm afraid his tales of adventure will be missed," continued Mr. Renton, "as will his expertise in finding and recovering important art treasures from the far corners of the globe."

"Yes," agreed the fat man. "I am quite aware of the exploits of the incredible Mr. Rigney. His adventures are legendary throughout the shadowy world of rascals, scamps, and treasure hunters. I am likewise impressed by not only the quality of his discoveries, but also the quantity. He was prolific, to say the least. Is that not so, Mr. Renton?"

"I commend you on your knowledge of the subject, Sir Arthur," gushed the glowing curator. "Yes, you are correct. Without the overwhelming and extremely generous contributions by Mr. Rigney, I'm afraid our museum would be little more than an indigent trading post dealing in locally crafted trinkets and baubles. Mr. Rigney's expertise and proficiency propelled Avalon's museum to a lofty position in the art world. He left us a legacy that will provide the museum with important treasures for years to come. In fact, we were forced to commandeer a large basement room at Bird Park so we would have the space to begin to catalog, house, and restore the bulk of treasure recovered by our patron."

"Fascinating, my friend," chimed the fat man. "Extremely fascinating, indeed."

"Perhaps Sir Arthur would like to see our restoration process some afternoon?" asked the gracious curator, offering a tour of the hen house to the fox.

"That would be delightful, Mr. Renton. That would be the highlight of my visit to this enchanting island. I look forward, with great anticipation, to your very generous invitation. That's very kind of you, Mr. Renton. I would be honored, sir. Very honored, indeed."

The fat man seemed cheerfully satisfied with himself and his inroads into the inner sanctum of Catalina's art repository. I would have to arrange for the rotund nobleman to be chaperoned on his tour with the naïve curator.

As the fat man prepared to take his leave, I accompanied him to the exit, and off-handedly inquired as to the whereabouts of his monolithic associate. The fat man responded that he was under the impression that Phangs Pa had taken up with a concubine and was engaged in carnal activities in Cooley Town.

Sir Arthur bid the spry curator, Mrs. Rigney, and myself a pleasant afternoon and was off at a brisk pace, destination unknown. Mrs. Rigney and I likewise bid farewell and good luck with the auction to the beaming Sumner Renton and were on our way to a quick lunch before we returned to the estate.

We walked the short distance from the museum back along the harbor to an outdoor restaurant overlooking the lolling boats and blue Pacific. We enjoyed a leisurely lunch of crab salad and, of course, champagne. I had come to realize that the reason for the unending supply of champagne was an attempt to conserve fresh water.

Sailboats lazily crisscrossed the harbor entrance, and pleasure boats of all sizes and descriptions casually bobbed at their moorings. The outspoken sea gulls circled overhead and occasionally dove beneath the surface of the water for herring, while squadrons of low-flying brown pelicans skimmed the surface of the waves.

While we dined, I asked Mrs. Rigney about the ownership of the museum and its relationship to the Rigney family. She explained that the museum was part of R.J.'s original vision for the casino. It was established through a trust set up by R.J.

and administered by a board of directors, of which she was a member. The museum, which also served as an art and auction gallery, was not directly a part of the Catalina Cattle Company or the gaming and entertainment venues. The museum and gallery were a separate entity, and must prosper or fail on their own.

She went on to explain that the museum had a standard exhibit that documented the history of the island, but it also served as an art gallery or auction house when it displayed consigned works by a renowned artist or a compilation of works dedicated to a specific theme or subject matter. P.K., for example, had provided a vast inventory of sunken treasure from around the world. Therefore, on some occasions, the museum would exhibit recovered artifacts from the Caribbean or off the coast of Madagascar in the Indian Ocean.

We finished our meal and relaxed over a cup of coffee. I decided to get some of the background homework out of the way and proceed to more pertinent investigation—motive. I asked Mrs. Rigney if she was aware of any recent addendum to R.J.'s will that might place one family member at a disadvantage, or produce resentment from the staff at the mansion.

She explained that the only change that had been made recently was to make her the executor of the estate because of her husband's disappearance, as he was the former executor. Beyond that, nothing had changed, and the will was all part of the family trust. The Commodore had had the family and corporate assets placed in a trust long ago. Furthermore, all family members, as well as house staff were well taken care of through the trust upon R.J.'s demise.

We finished our lunch and stepped back out onto the boardwalk, where we found Roscoe leaning on his cab, reading the paper. I helped Mrs. Rigney into the cab and asked Roscoe to drive her back to the estate. Upon his return to town, I asked that he retrieve me from the casino and then drive me back up to the estate as well.

The cab drove off toward the mansion, and I retraced our path along the boardwalk to the casino to check with Harry, the accountant geek.

Harry seemed piqued upon my arrival. He questioned my work ethics and became incensed when I explained where I had been and what I was doing for most of the afternoon.

"When I arrived here," he began, "I was under the impression that you were here to assist me. When I give you an assignment, Mr. Dugan, I expect you to carry out that assignment in due haste."

As he continued, his labored whisper became more of a hysterical tirade. He rose to his feet and came closer and closer, all the while shaking a hand full of papers nearer and nearer to my face. Once he had encroached on my "comfort zone," I slapped the papers from his hand and throttled him by his cheesy necktie. I shook him a couple of times then pulled his face close to mine, so that I stared straight into his eyes. He struggled on his tiptoes.

"Don't you ever get up in my face like that again," I said through clenched teeth. "I was hired for this job by the Rigney Corporation, not by your pansy little ass, Spanky. So keep your whining to yourself!"

I shoved him back into his chair and told him I would get the job done—just don't pull my chain about it.

"You choked me!" he said hysterically. "You didn't have to choke me, you crude, impetuous brute! You disgusting barbarian—you touched me! Why did you touch me? I don't like anybody to touch me! I'll never forgive you for that!" he said, almost in tears.

"Geeze! Take a pill, Harry." I felt sorry for the impudent little jerk. The way he was acting, though, you'd a thought I just roughed up his mother or something. That's just about how I felt, too. I went over and got him a Dixie cup of water from the office water cooler. "Here, Harry," I said, handing him the cup. "Calm down already. Don't get your panties in a wad. You just caught me off guard there for a second, man. Geeze, Harry, I didn't realize you were so impulsive."

I smoothed his shirt and straightened his tie. He looked down to where I futzed with his tie, and I tweaked his nose playfully. "I'll see you tomorrow morning at nine sharp," I said with a soft punch to his shoulder. I left to catch my ride back to the mansion, leaving him to pout on his own.

Chapter 8

The Auction

Mrs. Rigney and I returned to the museum at sunset. The interior had been transformed. The floor had been cleared of the artwork and replaced with rows of seating facing a raised platform opposite the entrance. Atop the platform was an auctioneer's podium.

The casino area was again a dazzling spectacle of glittering lights and excited anticipation. The casino was aglow, and the elegantly attired again gathered in impressive numbers for the evening's festivities.

Mrs. Rigney wore a simple, understated white satin dress, cut short above the knee and low at the neckline, topped by a single strand of pearls around her smooth, tanned neck. The thin straps over her beautiful, golden-brown shoulders bore witness to her movements beneath the thin shiny material, and a soft white shawl caressed her bare back. She was gorgeous and elegant, as always. I was again decked out in my dashing, borrowed, white dinner jacket. I was actually beginning to acquire the reddish glow of new sunburn on top of old saltwater tan. The two of us, in brilliantly radiant attire, were the picture of sublime island elegance.

The evening began with casual mingling, hor d'oeuvres, and of course, the virtual spring of bubbly. I mentioned the artesian wells of champagne theory to Mrs. Rigney, and she assured me that R.J. held the distribution rights for all distilled liquor, wine, and champagne on the island. But of course. She reminded me that the Commodore originally smuggled bootleg whiskey so, of course, he would be the incumbent regarding current distributing rights.

Finally, the esteemed curator, Sumner Renton, stepped to the podium and began the festivities, which were to include the auction and a complimentary dinner and dance upstairs in the ballroom.

"Good evening, ladies and gentlemen, welcome to Avalon and the paradise that is Santa Catalina Island. In keeping with our carnival theme, we are proud to present for auction this evening a body of artifacts discovered by our benevolent benefactor, the late Mr. P.K. Rigney. His adventurous spirit and legendary gallantry and bravado have made the Avalon Museum, and this evening's festivities, the cultural event it is today."

As the participants found their respective seats, Mr. Renton provided some historical background on the items to be auctioned. "Ladies and gentlemen, this evening's bounty is rich with history. Most of you know of the fascinating tale of Spanish Conquistadors and their plunder of Central and South America—the legend of the *San Roque*.

"The *San Roque* was the flagship of a fleet of twenty galleons returning to Spain that sunk within sight of Isle de la Bahia in the western Caribbean during a severe storm in the year 1606. Each of the galleons was laden with tons of gold and silver, according to the ship's manifest, which we also recovered. The manifest will remain among the museum's permanent collection, along with a select number of items from among the recovered treasures.

"According to the *San Roque's* manifest," he continued, "one ship alone carried one hundred and eighty chests of gold and silver coins, five hundred and twenty bars of silver, one hundred gold ingots, and one thousand pounds of gold leaf."

An audible gasp was heard throughout the room. Nearly everyone in the gallery turned and whispered to their neighbor. I looked at Mrs. Rigney, and the grin on her face indicated her pleasure with the excitement and surprise at the fortune imagined of the *San Roque*. The curator was positively giddy with the exuberance generated in the audience.

"Now, ladies and gentleman," he continued. "I am not at liberty to disclose the total amount of the bounty we were able to recover and return to Avalon. Unfortunately, the Honduran government now lays territorial claim upon the islands off which the *San Roque* lies. The *San Roque* and other gold and silver-laden galleons of the fleet lie under only twenty-two feet of water. It requires only a diving mask and snorkel to recover millions of dollars worth of sunken treasure."

Once again, a hushed murmur spread through the assembled masses. Anticipation grew with realization of the significance of the items offered for bidding this evening.

Sumner Renton raised his arms to calm the excitement building among the art connoisseurs. "Now, my friends," he said, "at this moment, the Honduran Navy has several coastal patrol vessels anchored over the *San Roque*, keeping curiosity seekers well away from the fortune lying just under the surface of the water. Therefore, I needn't explain the importance of this evening's festivities. This may be your only opportunity to acquire artifacts recovered from the *San Roque*." A heightened state of anticipation gripped the crowd.

"Before we begin tonight's auction," said Renton, "I would like to express our gratitude to the museum's board of directors and the Rigney family for their support, both of which are represented this evening by Mrs. Lara Rigney." He motioned to where Mrs. Rigney and I stood at the back of the room. The crowd responded with spontaneous applause, and Mrs. Rigney acknowledged their appreciation with a slightly embarrassed and humble curtsy.

"Now, ladies and gentlemen, without further ado," announced the excited curator, "let the festivities begin!"

The auctioneer stepped up to the podium with a small entourage of assistants. Several spotters lined the front of the stage, and several more lined either side of the room to assist the auctioneer in recognizing and identifying bidding participants. Other assistants were stationed off-stage to coordinate and deliver on-stage the items as they went up for bid.

With a sharp whack of the gavel, the first items arrived on stage. "Ladies and gentlemen," the auctioneer began. "The first items up for bid, referred to in your catalog as Lot Number One—one hundred gold coins in pristine condition. Who will start the bidding at ten thousand dollars?"

Numbered bidding paddles rose into the air, and the spotters began to point with one hand while waving to the auctioneer with the other. The bidding was on and continued at a brisk, only slightly subdued pace. The room was kinetic and the excited participants struggled to retain a modicum of composure. As the bidding progressed, I gazed around the room to see who had honored us with their presence this evening.

The fat man, Sir Arthur Sydney, was in attendance, without his apparently indisposed Chinese monolith. The dashing Blaine Pond was also present in the back, seemingly more interested in the attendees than the items being auctioned at the front of the room. As I watched, he continually scanned the crowd. He paid very little attention to the artifacts displayed on stage, but instead appeared to be making a mental inventory of specific individuals amongst the gathered masses. I tried to follow his gaze from one person to another. There was the fat man, of course. His size alone made him obvious. He then looked to an imperious, stalwart Chinese gentleman dressed in a traditional jacket that buttoned up the front to a stiff, short collar. The man, though small in stature, appeared sturdy, with a wiry quickness and agility. Resolute and uncompromising, his features were drawn tightly over high cheekbones, and he was well manicured, stylishly groomed.

The diminutive Chinese gentleman expressionlessly studied the items being displayed. However, I noticed that occasionally he, too, took inventory of individuals in the room. There was more rubbernecking going on here than at a tennis match at a nudist colony.

I continued to follow Mr. Pond's scan to another Chinese man. This one was rather portly, dressed in a seersucker suit and

Panama hat. He wore a Fu Manchu mustache and carried a distinctive ebony cane, the handle of which was an intricately carved golden dragon. Another Chinaman, dressed in a finely tailored and expensive western business suit, accompanied him. He possessed an inner strength—a certain self-confidence. He seemed darkly sinister—evil, somehow.

I watched Mr. Pond's inspection and noted the individuals in which he seemed interested. Inadvertently, our eyes met. We each gave a slight nod of acknowledgement and then returned our attention to the podium, feigning interest.

I leaned toward Mrs. Rigney and asked in a low whisper if she was acquainted with either of the Chinese gentlemen in which Mr. Pond interested. She gazed around the room to where my eyes led. She whispered that she was not acquainted with the portly man in the white suit or his companion, but that the stoic and shiny Chinaman was none other than the infamous Dr. Con, who owned the bat guano mining operation on the far side of the island.

Mrs. Rigney motioned me toward the exit and asked if I would like a breath of fresh air. We strolled to the sea wall and gazed over the serene harbor. I lit her cigarette and one for myself.

"Dr. Con," she began, "is an extremely secretive man. There is a virtual paramilitancy surrounding his operation. You may not have noticed yesterday during our tour, but an extremely vigilant cadre of very loyal and highly motivated Chinese guards patrols the area constantly. They escort any interlopers from the area. Entrance to the harbor is vigorously restricted."

Naturally, I asked why Dr. Con was so paranoid.

"The necessity for such extreme security measures, according to Dr. Con," she explained, "is that the operation is only conducted at night, when the bats are outside the cave feeding. The mining is suspended during the daylight hours following the bats' return in the early morning. Dr. Con insists that the bats remain undisturbed during the day to preserve the colony.

That is why he allows no one near the compound in the day-time. At night, he says, it is far too dangerous for anyone to venture near the harbor area because of the constant tugboat traffic in and out of the harbor entrance.

"He has been trying for years to secure a dredging permit from the island's Conservancy Commission, to dredge the har-bor at Smuggler's Cove to a depth that would accommodate large container vessels in which to transport his product in lar-ger amounts. The environmental concerns have thus far prevented him from acquiring the necessary permission. The struggle has created very harsh feelings in some of the locals; there is no love lost between Dr. Con and a large segment of the island's inhabitants. There are even rumored suspicions of late that Dr. Con is clandestinely dredging the harbor anyway, using underwater divers and a sluice machine that sucks sand and eve-rything else off the bottom and deposits it somewhere else. The Conservancy has been monitoring the build-up of silt and sedi-mentary deposits along the coast south of the harbor, and recording the intrusion of these sediments in Seal Cove and the sea lion habitat. The Conservancy considers dredging a serious threat to the delicate ecosystem of the island, and it has waged a heated battle with Dr. Con for some time. That, no doubt," she concluded, "is another reason why Dr. Con allows no trespass-ers near the area. It has become a divisive issue amongst the islanders and the people associated with Dr. Con's operation. He's not making any friends among the locals, that's for sure."

Mrs. Rigney and I returned to the throes of the museum's auction. Bidding continued as the auctioneer displayed weap-onry and armor recovered from the sunken galleons. Helmets, swords, cannon, ship's anchors, bells, and other nautical accou-trements were swept up with as much enthusiasm as the finer examples of jewelry, ceramics, and priceless works of art in sil-ver and gold.

The auction appeared an overwhelming success and the en-thusiasm of the participants was contagious. The room was abuzz with excitement, and everyone, especially the beaming curator, appeared to find the evening's events satisfying.

Upon the conclusion of the auction, everyone was invited upstairs to the ballroom for dining and dancing. As the crowd began to exit the museum, I tried to observe who was following whom.

Dr. Con slipped quietly from the proceedings and was whisked away in an imposing black limousine. Mr. Pond hailed a cab and was off in the same direction, followed him.

The portly Chinese gentleman and his smarmy sidekick didn't seem to be in any hurry; they lingered outside, watching the masses and whispering amongst themselves. Inspector La-Farge was on hand outside with one of his officers, keeping a mental diary of the honored guests' comings and goings.

Sir Arthur eventually emerged from the museum after conferring with the curator, presumably regarding the trinkets and baubles he had bid on successfully. Once outside, he made a beeline for the buffet table in the ballroom.

Inside the museum, and all around the casino, was a large contingent of Pinkerton guards and plainclothes detectives. It was a comforting presence, considering the small fortune housed by the museum. There was also the matter of the change of ownership for the auctioned items and the transfer of purchases off the island by each buyer. Having Pinkertons on the job was someone's very good idea.

Mrs. Rigney and I walked the short distance to the entrance of the ballroom. Tonight, a lavish buffet had been set out with a vast array of sumptuous delicacies. An enchanted evening of dining and dancing ensued, punctuated by laughter and animated conversations about the afternoon's fantasy treasure romp. Everyone was engaged in an anecdotal tale about this precious item, or that magnificent work of art, caught up in an atmosphere of mass cultural aphrodisiac. It was an enchanting evening and all in attendance were flush with spirit and spirits.

After successfully navigating the buffet table more than once, I set my over-stuffed course toward the bar. I plopped my sagging girth onto an available bar stool and ordered a straight shot, my first since arriving on the island. I tipped my head back and slammed it down. I placed the shot glass back on the bar and exhaled heavily with warm, glowing satisfaction.

"Excuse me, Mr. Dugan. Please excuse the interruption," said the smarmy Chinaman with a wide grin. "Perhaps I could persuade you to join my associate and me for refreshments at our table." He motioned to where the portly Chinaman in white sat.

"I suppose I could be persuaded," I said, lifting myself off the barstool. "Bring the bottle."

As he reached across the bar for the bottle, I caught a glimpse of the tattoo on the inside of his forearm. It was an in-tricately designed, brilliantly colored tattoo of a fire-breathing dragon. I'd seen identical tattoos many times before in China-town. He was a Tong. Chinese Mafia. Extremely vicious, very brutal.

The Tong preyed predominantly upon fearful Chinese im-migrants in Chinatown and surrounding neighborhoods. They controlled criminal activities such as prostitution, drugs, and extortion with cruel efficiency. Police investigations in China-town rarely progressed very far; the population is terrified of Tong reprisals and therefore tight-lipped and unwilling to even speak to the police. They never see anything, and they never know anything. "No speaky Engleesh."

The Chinaman in white stood and bowed upon my arrival. He smiled warmly and offered his hand. "Mr. Dugan, sir," he began. "Very humble to make your honorable acquaintance. Please join us. Let me offer you refreshment. Please allow me to present my esteemed associate, Ahn Hai."

Ahn Hai was not his family name. I was familiar enough with the Chinese under-world to know that Ahn Hai meant "Big Brother"—a term of respect similar to that of La Cosa Nostra's

Godfather, or "Don." It signified a position of respect. He was one to be feared in the criminal organization.

"Mr. Dugan, sir," began the Chinaman. "My name is Chang, Qui-Kane Chang. My associate and I represent the Nationalist government of China. I humbly beg that you forgive my abruptness, Mr. Dugan, sir, but I realize that you are a busy man; therefore, I shall not waste your valuable time with idle small talk or quaint Chinese proverbs." That was refreshing.

"It is our understanding that you are a private investigator, currently employed by the Rigney Corporation for an accounting audit. Is that not so, Mr. Dugan, sir?" he asked.

"First of all, my friend," I responded, "I may or may not be currently employed. I may be here strictly on vacation. I'm sure you will enlighten me as to how it is any concern of yours. Secondly, I'm not sure I was aware that the government of Formosa retained the Tong as official diplomatic emissaries."

Ahn Hai seemed to think that that was pretty funny, judging by the sneer that attempted to form a smile.

"Mr. Dugan, sir," retorted Chang. "The choice of assistants was my own discretion, not my government's. I required someone who knew his way around the Los Angeles area. Ahn Hai certainly meets that requirement, and he has a familiarity with the culture and language. He also provides a certain amount of personal security in unfamiliar territory. Mr. Dugan, sir," he continued, "I shall get to the point. I wish to retain your services to recover a work of art that was secreted from our territorial waters and for which we have reason to believe has found its way to this island."

"This work of art must be pretty valuable for your government to send you halfway around the world, to recover it."

"Monetarily," he explained, "the value is negligible. However, culturally, the item is held in high esteem. Its value lies in its ancestral heritage. Its value would be the same as the value of your country's Liberty Bell. It is worth virtually nothing, but it is priceless in the hearts and heritage of the people who have defended its honor."

"What exactly is the work of art for which you are searching?" I asked.

"Are we agreed, then, that you will represent us in our quest, Mr. Dugan, sir?"

"No, I haven't agreed to anything yet. If your assumption is correct, I am already retained, and therefore could not afford the time your project would require. If, however, I am not currently employed and merely here on vacation, I would not be inclined to accept an invitation for employment."

"Mr. Dugan, sir," implored Mr. Chang, "this is a very important matter in the eyes of my government and in the hearts of my countrymen. Time is of the essence. I am authorized to offer you, on behalf of my government, an amount equal to double your normal rate, plus a generous finder's fee upon successfully taking possession of the item in question. Either way, Mr. Dugan, sir," he said, "whether previously retained or on vacation, we are prepared to make it worth your while. I believe that is the correct phrase."

I slammed another shot and sat staring at the empty glass in quiet contemplation. I was hammered. "Mr. Chang, I am willing to entertain your proposal, but I return to my previously unanswered question. What is it, exactly, that you are searching for?"

The portly Mr. Chang leaned back in his chair and gave a sidelong glance to his smarmy associate. I quietly slid my hand under my jacket and unsnapped my .38. I wasn't sure what Mutt and Jeff had in mind, but I was prepared for the worst.

"Very well, Mr. Dugan, sir," the portly gentleman finally acquiesced. "I will tell you what we are looking for. But I must quote one of your proverbs—discretion is the better part of valor. Are you familiar with that term, Mr. Dugan?"

I released the grip on my equalizer and breathed an inaudible sigh of relief. "Yes, I'm familiar with that term," I responded. "'Discretion is the better part of valor' is my middle name. That's why I want to know what you're looking for before I get in over my head."

I sensed that I was already getting in over my head with the straight shots I was throwing back. I was beginning to get a little fuzzy. Next would come belligerence, then melancholy. If I survived belligerence and kept drinking, melancholy would be followed by the dreaded double P's—puking and passing out.

Mr. Chang leaned forward and spoke quickly, but directly. "Mr. Dugan, sir, we are searching for a statuette about two feet tall. It is made of lead, overlaid in gold leaf, and depicts a fire-breathing dragon in an upright, defensive posture." He held up his ebony cane with the golden dragon handle that I had taken note of earlier at the auction.

"This is a one-quarter scale replica of the statuette in question. As you can see, the eyes are rubies and the spine plates and claws are presented in emeralds."

"Yes," I said. "I was admiring your cane at the auction. That's very distinctive head piece."

"There is one other item, Mr. Dugan, sir," interrupted Chang. "A bronze seal accompanies the golden dragon. The seal attests to the statuette's authenticity—it is from the time of the Zhi Yan dynasty in the fourteenth century. We, of course, wish to recover this item, as well."

"And what makes you think that the dragon is on this island?" I asked.

Chang once again leaned back in his chair, but instead of glancing at his companion, he looked across the room to where Sir Arthur appeared to be taking interest in our conversation. Chang leaned forward again and spoke softly. "We have reason to believe that the late Mr. P.K. Rigney may have recovered these items between the island of Takashima and the waters near the East China Sea, during his final expedition. Through our contacts we have traced the golden dragon and the bronze seal over many surreptitious routes to precisely this charming island," he said.

"Well, Mr. Chang," I finally said, "that's a very interesting story. I can certainly see how these items would be important to your people's heritage. You don't mind if I sleep on it tonight and let you know my answer tomorrow, do you?" I asked. "It's past my bedtime, and I need to think about it for a bit."

Mr. Chang stared deep into my eyes, studying me. "Very well, Mr. Dugan, sir," he finally said. "Contemplation is good for the soul. My people have waited six centuries to recover the golden dragon; a few more hours will do no harm. I must caution you, however, Mr. Dugan, sir—time is of the essence; the jackals have already begun to converge." Once again, he glanced over to where the fat man nonchalantly sipped cognac and inconspicuously tried his damnedest to read our lips.

"Okay, Mr. Chang," I said as I got up from my chair. "Until we meet again. I hope you enjoy your stay on the island, and I hope you're successful in your quest for the statue." We curtly bowed to one another then I, with some difficulty, found my way back to where Mrs. Rigney waited at our table.

"You left me unattended again, Dugan," she said upon my return. "This is becoming quite an unattractive habit with you, and I'm beginning to feel very neglected."

"I'm sorry, angel," I said. "You certainly deserve my undivided attention, but take comfort in the knowledge that I am on the job and at long last seem to be making some headway." She looked at me quizzically.

"I'll explain later," I said. "There appears to be attention gravitating on me from some very diverse sources. For now, let me ask you—do you have any knowledge of a statuette, a golden dragon encrusted with rubies and emeralds, here on the island? It may have been recovered by P.K. on his last expedition, and secreted back to Avalon." She sat in quiet contemplation for a moment with wrinkled brow.

"No," she finally said. "I don't know anything about a golden dragon."

Chapter 9

The Blue Parrot

Mrs. Rigney and I found Roscoe leaning on his cab in the usual spot outside the casino. He drove us back to the estate and up the palm-lined drive to the mansion. She went inside to check on the Commodore, then with a wave goodnight, retired for the evening.

We had returned to the estate just after the changing of the guard. Bogie and his handler were patrolling the grounds through the night and into the early morning. The fact that Bogie was prowling the area in the dark didn't comfort Roscoe. He seemed uneasy knowing that Bogie was out there, lurking in the shadows. He remained in his cab with the windows rolled up and the doors locked until I returned for the trip back to town.

Before leaving again, I checked on the family and staff's whereabouts and tomorrow's itineraries. Everyone was settled for the evening, except Rita Rigney. She was always the last one through the gates in the evening or the early hours of the morning. She enjoyed her nightlife.

Roscoe drove me back to town. During the ride, we talked about the festivities taking place on the island and how everyone looked forward to the excitement of this week. For the locals, it was the beginning of the summer tourist season and the start of long hours and big bucks. For the tourists and the international 'hoi polloi,' it was the inaugural bash of the social season, and a chance to get out there and enjoy the best money could buy and the thrills that life had to offer.

For shiny new debutantes, it was their initial sojourn into the world of boys, dating, and sex. They were no longer sunburned children frolicking on the sandy shore, laughing with innocent delight as they ran from the ebb and flow of the gently caressing waves. Now they tingled with adolescent anticipation. It was an exciting time in their young lives. They danced, giggled, and timidly tested the threshold over which they would explore their right of passage.

For the taut and tanned twenty-something playboys and girls, the bouncy and flirtatious sun bucks and sand bunnies, this week marked the start of the party circuit in the fast lane of the sun-drenched tropical autobahns. During the winter months, they were forced to huddle together in ski lodges by warm fireplaces on forlorn mountaintops somewhere on the jet-set globe. They endured the perils of migrating from one posh resort to another. This week signaled the beginning of the season that included yachts, warm ocean waters, and cool evening breezes. Catalina was the place to enjoy all those things. This was "wet dream" island.

The comfortable, disposable income, middle-aged couples found Catalina the pristine tropical romance land they had worked all year to enjoy for a few brief days. The women approached their sexual peak as the boat approached the island, and the men wielded 'weapons of steel' as they cavorted around this exotically unencumbered paradise.

And for the old timers in the sunset of life, Catalina was a nostalgic stroll through the golden days of yesteryear—the days of flappers, Prohibition, burlesque revues, speakeasies, bootleg whiskey, and bathtub gin. The Golden Age of Hollywood took place only twenty-six miles away, and Avalon was always an adventurous weekend getaway for the rich and famous. Roscoe had seen them all. From Fatty Arbuckle to Adolph Zucker.

The Blue Parrot was what one would expect for a cocktail and dinner joint in this locale—lots of bamboo, rattan, and tall, colorful drinks with bright swizzles and festive umbrellas sticking out of them. The restaurant sat atop a row of shops overlooking the boardwalk and harbor. The wide, expansive windows in front were lined with comfortable, well-worn booths. On the back wall was a large, well-stocked rattan bar, busily manned by Hawaiian-shirted bartenders and waitresses in flowered sarongs and orchid leis.

I sat at the bar and ordered another straight shot. My level of belligerence had not yet risen to the annoying heights to which I was normally accustomed during these bouts of self-doubt. Usually, when I get like this (and for the life of me I don't know why), I get smashed, get into an altercation, about half the time get the crap kicked out of me, then spend the remainder of the evening whining about what a jerk I am and how I screwed up my life. Lots of fun for everyone involved.

The Blue Parrot, apparently, was the local watering hole for fashionable, upscale criminal types that find their way to the island. It was one rung up the clientele ladder from the scalawags and scoundrels one found at the Marlin Club. The well-dressed psychopaths engaged in hushed conversations seemed to be hucksters and hustlers, card cheats and loan sharks, larcenists, embezzlers, and thieves of all sizes and descriptions. I felt right at home.

About this time, I had reached surly on my personal inebriation meter and decided I'd better change my attitude and thought patterns before I got myself into trouble. I attempted to reassemble the list of suspects I accumulated in Johnny Rigney's disappearance. Besides the ones I had already put a tail on, I could now add Mr. Chang and his creepy companion Ahn Hai. The story they related to me could certainly be a motive, if Johnny actually had possession of the golden dragon.

There was also a growing list of interesting bit players perhaps involved. I still hadn't figured out what the dashing Blaine Pond was doing here. I just didn't buy the East-Asian Trading Company front. And then there was the infamous Dr. Con that Pond seemed so interested in. He could very well figure into this, although I couldn't begin to imagine how. I had come to realize that I really didn't know very damned much. I was getting nowhere fast. It seemed like I was pedaling my ass off on a bike with no chain, going through the motions, but not getting anywhere. Maybe I was not smart enough to get ahead of these people, much less keep up. I could be in way over my head. I didn't seem to be up to speed with this social stratum. I always seemed to be a little bit better than the average guy at whatever I did, but I never seemed to be the best. I was always good, but never number one. And then my thoughts drifted to Lara Rigney. Gorgeous, intelligent, arousing, and completely out of my league.

Well, I apparently passed through Belligerence Ville and was headed to Melancholy City. Next stop, the end of the line—puking and passing out. Just then, Sir Arthur Sidney entered the establishment, searching for someone, I guessed from his mannerism. He eventually spotted me and hastened to where I sat.

"Ah, Mr. Dugan," he said cheerfully. "Just the man I was looking for. Can I buy you a drink, my friend?"

Without waiting for my reply, he motioned to the bartender to bring two more of what I was having.

"Mr. Dugan, I wonder if I might have a word with you in private?" he asked motioning to a booth in the corner.

Another drink was not what I really needed, but I guessed I could hold myself together long enough to find out what the fat man had on his mind. We picked up our drinks and moved to the booth. He wasted no time with pleasantries and began straightaway.

"Mr. Dugan, it has come to my attention that you are in possession of a certain inventory list. That being the case, I wondered if you might allow me to quickly peruse it."

"Well, Sir Arthur," I said, "let's assume for the moment that I indeed have the list. I'm not saying that I do, but just for fun, let's assume I have the list. What would you be looking for?"

"Come, come, my friend," he began. "Surely you realize that there are a good number of objects d' art that I am continually in search of, no matter my immediate quest. I merely hope I might spot something on your list that I might reserve the first right of refusal upon. I assure you, my friend, that my intentions are honorable. As I stated at our first meeting, I have a certain recognizable talent for finding that bit of treasure amongst the flotsam and jetsam. The diamond in the rough, if you will. I'm merely seeking a perfectly 'legit'—I believe that is the correct vernacular—business opportunity."

I had almost forgotten about the list and resisted the impulse to reach in my pocket for it. I was reasonably certain I had placed the list and ring of keys in the pocket of the jacket I was wearing.

"I'm afraid, if I had such a list, it would fall into the category of client confidentiality," I responded. "It wouldn't be prudent of me to allow you to see the list. Hypothetically speaking, of course."

He smiled broadly, and then continued. "Perhaps, if you are not inclined to grant my first request, you would be agreeable to a business proposition?" he asked.

"Depends on the proposition and what's in it for me," I said.

"Aha!" The fat man laughed aloud. "Cut right to the chase. Yes, I do enjoy that fabulous American characteristic, yes indeed, I do. You never cease to amaze me, Mr. Dugan. Yes, I do enjoy your straight forward, no frills approach to life. No beating around the bush. What you see is what you get. Take it or leave it. Yes, very entertaining, Mr. Dugan."

"You know, you're slicker 'n hot shit sliding through a tin horn," I said. "Why don't we cut the crap and skip the cliché-fest. What is it you want, Artie?" I asked.

"Ahhh!" he burst out laughing again. "Now there's one I haven't heard before." He removed a pen from his vest pocket and wrote my inebriated diatribe on a cocktail napkin for posterity. "'Hot-shit through a tin horn,'" he repeated and laughed heartily until his face was flushed. The boisterous laughter degenerated to an uncontrollable coughing binge. He downed a shot that straightened him right up and allowed him to regain his composure.

"Oh, Mr. Dugan," the fat man finally said, "you are a character, sir. You really are an entertaining chap, I must say. Indeed, you are, my friend. I look forward to the day we might sit down with a good bottle and swap tales of intrigue and lust. I certainly hope that we might do just that some day, my friend. Indeed, I do."

"Very well, my friend," the fat man said. "I shall tell you precisely what I'm searching for, and you can decide if you wish to cooperate or not. However, I must insist that you keep the information I am about to divulge to yourself—not only to insure the confidentiality of my purpose, but for your own safety, as well as that of the Rigney family. You see, there are vultures circling about as we speak. Grisly beasts. So vulgar and uncouth. They are barbaric individuals, prone to attack and squabble amongst themselves for the most grotesque considerations. Be very careful, my friend. As they say, it is a jungle out there." The fat man giggled to himself then ordered another round. "If you will indulge me for a short while," he said, "I shall provide some pertinent historical facts, so you might realize the significance of the objects in question. Are you familiar with the thirteenth-century reign of the Mongolian emperor Kubla Khan, Mr. Dugan?"

"No, I'm afraid my grasp of ancient Chinese history is tenuous at best," I responded.

"Kubla Khan was the grandson of the infamous Mongolian conqueror Genghis Khan and possessed the same plundering ambitions," the fat man began. "In 1268, having conquered northern China and Korea, Kubla Khan demanded submission from Japan. The Japanese ignored the command, and the Khan prepared to invade their island stronghold. Finally, in November 1274, a fleet of 900 ships and 40,000 Mongolian, Chinese, and Korean troops arrived at Kyushu's Hakata Bay. Kyushu is the most southwesterly island stronghold of the Japanese Empire.

"After a day's successful fighting, the invaders retired for the night. But that evening, a storm threatened the fleet at anchor, forcing the ship captains to put to sea. The storm eventually overtook the fleet, sinking 200 ships; the total cost in lives was 13,500.

"Despite the toll, Kubla Khan prepared another attack. By the spring of 1281, a vast armada consisting of 4,400 ships and 142,000 Mongolian, Chinese, and Korean troops began assembling in Chinese and Korean ports for a second assault of Japan. By contrast, Mr. Dugan," the fat man continued, "the famed Spanish armada three centuries later numbered only 130 ships and 27,500 men. A paltry number by comparison. You can imagine the vast numbers of ships and men involved.

"This time, however, the Japanese were well prepared. In the seven-year interval, they had built an immense wall around Hakata Bay, a massive structure some 2.5 meters high and 20 kilometers long. The Mongols apparently had no knowledge of the wall because they landed the advance portion of their army directly in front of it. The close quarters robbed them of their most successful tactic, the lightning cavalry charge that had routed the finest armies of Asia and Eastern Europe.

"The two armies were closely matched, and skirmishes raged around Hakata Bay. Neither side could gain a clear advantage, and the invaders were forced to retreat to their ships and sail westward out of the bay. Toward the end of July, the force attacked the island of Takashima, southwest of Hakata Bay, and conquered it. Meanwhile, the emperor of Japan and other high-ranking officials sought the aid of the gods, performing elaborated Shinto ceremonies at shrines throughout the country on behalf of the defending army. As if in answer to their prayers, the Divine Wind, or Kamikaze, struck the Takashima area in August, with devastating effect.

"Many of the fleet's finest vessels were sunk at anchor when the storm struck. Others were swept ashore and bashed to bits by the fierce ocean. Some of the fleet, however, managed to set sail and escape destruction in the open ocean southwest, toward the East China Sea." The fat man was noticeably excited by the story and leaned across the table and spoke in more hushed tones.

"At this point, my friend," said the fat man, "the legend of the Lost Fleet of Kubla Khan becomes murky and fascinating. You see, Mr. Dugan," he continued, "the bedraggled and tattered remains of the once-magnificent fleet escaped the devastation of the Kamikaze only to be set upon by pirates in the open ocean of the East China Sea.

"There are some," he continued, "who hold to the theory that the pirates simply attacked and sunk the haggard fleet, sending the remaining spoils of their Japanese plunder to the bottom. There is another theory, however, that gives credence to the idea that the pirates attacked the Mongols, captured the remaining vessels, and took possession of the treasures. I believe, Mr. Dugan, that indications in certain historical documents confirm the latter theory."

I began to sense a convergence of interests. Even in my dulled state, I realized that Mr. Chang and Sir Arthur were on a quest for the same treasure—the treasure that the late P.K. Rigney tried so valiantly to conceal. That was, likewise, why Sir Arthur seemed so overly concerned with the conversation between Mr. Chang and myself at the casino earlier this evening.

"You see my friend," the fat man continued, "I am aware of certain authenticated documentation that would lead one who was skilled in such things to believe that a legendary pirate based in Macau, by the name of Quo Sing Ye, boasted of possessing specific artifacts known to have come from the ill-fated fleet in the year 1569.

"Later, a renowned woman pirate called the Widow Ching was known to be in possession of certain items from the same treasure. In 1848, at the end of the Opium Wars, the Chinese emperor utilized the power of the British Royal Navy to drive away the notorious Pirate Choo Ya Poo, for which the British were rewarded with territorial claim over what is now colonial Hong Kong. It is believed that Choo Ya Poo had in his possession the Khan's treasure. The British Navy chased him across the sea to virtually the same location between the East China Sea and the island of Takashima, where the Khan's original invasion fleet had been sunk or captured nearly six centuries before, and there sank Choo's entire fleet of ships, sending them to the bottom, virtually on top of the original Mongolian armada.

"It is at this point in the story," said the fat man, "you and Mr. Chang have already conversed. Is that not true, Mr. Dugan?"

"So, I see you can indeed read lips, my assiduous friend," I said.

The fat man chuckled with delight. "To take a cue from your previous answer, my friend, maybe I do and maybe I don't. At any rate, I must caution you against entering into an alliance with the infamous Mr. Chang. Mr. Chang and I are contemporaries of sort," he continued. "We have crossed paths throughout the world on occasion. I would not be inclined to put much faith in any verbal contract or guarantee he might offer. Though he seems honorable, I would wager that he would slit his own grandmother's throat to get what he wants. Be very careful, my friend."

"So what do you say, my friend?" asked the fat man. "Do we have a basis upon which to consummate a business arrangement? I can hire you professionally and pay whatever rate is agreed upon or we could negotiate an arrangement based on cooperation, with a substantial percentage or a finder's fee, if we are successful in our quest. I am open to any suggestion you might have in mind. I do not object to negotiation, my friend."

I slumped in the booth and said nothing for a moment. I felt disheveled and a bit fuzzy around the edges. "No, I imagine that you do not object to negotiation, my long-winded friend; I rather suspect that you thrive upon it. Perhaps you won't object if I sleep on it tonight and get back to you tomorrow?"

A wide grin formed slowly on his abundant face. "I have no objection to that, sir," responded the fat man. "That would be satisfactory. I commend you on your astute business acumen, my friend. Yes, indeed, we must weigh the pros and cons, as it were, before entering into an agreement. Very well then, my friend. I believe that concludes our business for this evening." The Fat Man got up to leave. "I shall look forward to seeing you tomorrow, Mr. Dugan."

"Just a moment, Sir Arthur," I said. "You still have not told me what you're looking for."

"I was under the impression that Mr. Chang had already informed you as to what we're looking for," responded the fat man as he regained his seat.

"Yes," I said. "Mr. Chang told me what he was looking for, but as yet you have not. Maybe you and he are on a quest for different things."

"Yes, of course, very well," said the fat man. "I am looking for a statuette of a golden dragon that stands about this high and looks remarkably like the top of Mr. Chang's cane. A bronze seal accompanies the dragon. Does that correspond with what Mr. Chang revealed to you, my friend?"

"Yes, it appears as though you both are on a similar quest. However, he gave no indication as to their worth."

"Yes, well, that is a very good question and the subject of much speculation," responded the fat man. "If I were to speculate—obviously, they're worth many hundreds of thousands of dollars. Otherwise, neither Mr. Chang nor I would be particularly interested. However, my friend, with regard to the mystique that surrounds these unique items, they may be worth millions to the right party. You see, my friend, there may be some question as to the origins of some of the items known to be aboard the original ill-fated fleet. However, with regard to the bronze seal, my friend, there can be no question as to its origin. Emperor Kubla Khan requisitioned the inscription on the seal from a monk by the name of Phangs Pa. I see you recognize the name. The monk that produced the inscription on the bronze seal all those centuries ago was indeed an ancestor of my gigantic, though erudite friend.

"The unique historical significance of the bronze seal, my friend, is that it represents the first written Chinese language. Prior to 1274, when the seal was cast, there was no written language in China. Beyond that," continued Sir Arthur, "the inscription on the seal itself authenticates its origination as during the reign of the Zhi-Yuan Dynasty, an era we know encompasses that of Emperor Kubla Khan.

"The golden dragon is another matter entirely," he said. "There is some question as to whether the dragon was brought to Japan by Mongolian invaders or taken as a spoil of conquest from the Shinto shrine on the island of Takashima when it was conquered and held by Khan's armies. That, my suspicious friend, is why I would like to see the items described on your inventory list. You see," he continued, "I may be able to gain insight as to the origins of the golden dragon if I could inspect other items that were recovered from the same location. If there are artifacts indeed of Japanese origin, one could speculate as to the likelihood that the dragon was of similar origins. However, if the remainder of the recovered items were of Chinese origin exclusively, it would be prudent to surmise the golden dragon to be likewise. You see, Mr. Dugan," he said with obvious delight, "I told you it was a fascinating story, did I not?

"Together, my friend, we could solve a centuries old mystery and become stinking rich, all at the same time. Ahhh, what could be more thrilling and monetarily satisfying, my disheveled comrade? You could be rich and famous. You could be the man of the hour. You could be Lara Rigney's hero. And so my friend," said the fat man with obvious pleasure, "I believe I've salted the mine. Dangled a few carrots and fanned the flames of intrigue, as they say. I believe I've perked your interest, piqued your curiosity enough for this evening. Therefore, until tomorrow, my friend, I bid you adieu." With that, the fat man turned and skipped, Chaplinesque, from the Blue Parrot.

Chapter 10

Room Service, the Wake-Up Call

I motioned to the bartender for another shot. This would be my fourth or fifth for the evening. I lost count after two. I sat slumped in the warm leather pouch I had created in the booth, gazing out over the sleepy harbor. It was hard to imagine conspiratorial intrigue swirling around the tranquil little island. *It's a damn good thing I'm talking to myself*, I thought. I *would never, at this stage of inebriation, actually be able to pronounce the word 'conspiratorial' aloud.* I watched the reflection of myself in the window glass drunkenly laugh at my own pitiful joke. I looked pitiful. What a slotz. What a slob.

Suddenly there appeared, in the reflection behind my own, an angelic apparition. I turned from the window and gazed upon a beautiful, young, mixed-race Asian girl. She was around twenty-five. She had long dark hair and deep brown eyes—soft, doe-like. High, rounded cheekbones and a warm, shy smile. She stood at the end of the table holding a cup of hot coffee.

"Please excuse my impudence, Mr. Travis Dugan, sir," she begged in a warm, sweet voice. "I have brought you a cup of coffee rather than the drink you ordered. I hope that you will forgive me, but I humbly suggest a more prudent choice."

I'd never been eighty-sixed with such grace. "Thank you. I'm sorry; I don't know your name."

"My name is Chin Lee," she said with a bashful smile.

"Thank you, Chin Lee," I said. "You are wiser than your years would indicate. A cup of coffee would indeed be a more prudent choice."

She smiled brightly and set the coffee down in front of me. "I am off work in a little while," she said, "as soon as I clean up. Would you be kind enough to walk me home?"

"I would be honored to escort you home, Chin Lee. And thank you again for your concern for my well-being."

She gently patted the back of my hand before going off to close. The bus boys put the chairs on top of the tables after the waitresses wiped them off. Likewise, the bar stools, once the bartenders had swabbed the top of the bar. They re-filled ice receptacles, replenished cocktail napkins, washed shot glasses, and whatever else was required.

I sat quietly, sipping my coffee and vaguely contemplating the course of my investigation. It seemed to be gaining momentum towards some mysterious Chinese treasure. The world was full of uncertainty.

Once again, Chin Lee appeared at the end of my table. She had replaced the leis around her shoulders with a light sweater. A small purse hung from her arm; she appeared ready to go.

We descended the stairs of the Blue Parrot and turned north once we were out on the boardwalk. It was a warm, balmy night, and we casually strolled along the harbor to Whitley Avenue. She was silent, though I got the feeling there was something she wanted to say.

We turned from the harbor and walked up a challengingly steep hill until we arrived at a modest, split-level flat just off the narrow street. She put her key in the lock and opened the door. She turned to me in the doorway with the eyes of a newborn fawn, looking vulnerable and fragile.

"Mr. Travis Dugan, sir, you are here to find Johnny?" She looked as if she were going to cry.

I searched for something comforting to say. Her obvious concern and the pain she was apparently attempting to contain, along with the intimacy with which she spoke of Johnny Rigney, left me at a loss for words.

"Did you know Johnny Rigney very well?" I finally asked.

"Yes, I knew him," she answered. "When we were children. We grew up together," she said haltingly, choking back tears.

"Technically, I'm here on other business," I said. "But I am making discreet inquires. Chin Lee, I will see what I can do. I will look into the matter; hopefully, I can help ease your pain."

She took my hand and gently kissed it. "You are very kind Mr. Travis Dugan, sir; I am most grateful. Please, be very careful." She stepped in the room and, holding back her tears, closed the door behind her.

I paused in the doorway, puzzled, dazed, and fuzzy. I was in need of sleep. I turned and walked back down the hill to the boardwalk. I turned north one more block and started up the street to Mrs. O'Malley's boarding house.

This case, like many others, was like a kid's game where you must connect a series of random dots in order to see the picture in its entirety. There were many dots in this puzzle. I hoped I had enough lead in my pencil to complete the picture. Oh, yes, I had a luncheon date with the devastating Rita Rigney tomorrow, or this afternoon, depending on the current time. At any rate, my performance may not be up to my usual caliber, judging by the way that I felt at present. I quickened my pace toward my room and the comfort of warm, soft bed.

After my combat orientation flight, or "cherry ride," in the B-26C (the original designation was the Douglas A-26, or attack aircraft), the plane went through many modifications. After WWII, under more conventional wartime conditions, it had a crew of four, the aircraft commander in the left seat, the pilot, or co-pilot in the right seat, the navigator/bombardier in the nose, and the radar operator in the mid-section.

Modifications, A and B were solid nosed. One incorporated a 20 mm cannon, the other had a cluster of 50 mm machine guns. The B026C had a clamshell Plexiglas nose for greater visibility, a Norden bombsight for precise, mid-altitude bombing accuracy, a large LORAN (long range aerial navigation) mounted on the right side, and a control panel for bomb doors, selection, release, arming, etcetera mounted on the left—very snug, confining, and efficient.

Harry Spiller, Captain, West Point graduate, and the AC of the mission, singled me out as we were walking off the flight line and asked if I would like to fly with him on subsequent missions. In this war, "fly with," was but one of the many euphemisms that denoted "the other guy" on a two-man crew. The other guy took off and landed in the right seat as the co-pilot. He navigated to, from, and north of the bomb line (the 38th parallel of latitude), was the target spotter, bombardier, anti-aircraft suppressor, and general guide dog on every mission, but was only a pilot in emergency situations, assuming he could get back to the controls or was already in the right seat when the AC was incapacitated. The only crew position this other guy never undertook was radar operator. Since the radar was located amidships, and only accessible from the outside and over the top of the aircraft, it would be a bit difficult during in-flight operations. He didn't swab out the aircraft after landing, either.

At any rate, Captain Spiller had noted on this mission that I didn't appear shaken by all the bombing and strafing runs, sat quietly strapped into the right seat, had no comments to make, and stayed out of the way. He seemed a damned good pilot and well above average in attitude and demeanor, so since I hadn't thus far been assigned, why not?

This was Korea, and the air in Korea was a helluva lot different from what I had just left in the Pacific, what seemed just a very short time ago. In the war against Japan, we flew B-29s in massive formations during daylight hours at high altitudes and dropped tons of bombs over a wide area or missed the target area completely. We had discovered the high-altitude Japanese jet stream. A vast, high-speed stream of air, generally from west to east, which when flown directly into it dropped the ground speed (rate of movement over the ground) to zero, or on occasion, slowly pushed the aircraft backwards, out over the Pacific Ocean.

Flying with the wind, or downwind, of the jet stream proved no solution at all. The speed of the B-29 coupled with the speed of the jet stream created ground speeds that the Norden bomb-sight, the best in the world, could not calculate fast enough to accomplish solutions, making it useless.

With the arrival of General Curtiss Lemay, "the Cigar" as the commander of the Twentieth Air Force, changes were in the offing—lower altitudes, fewer and lower daylight strikes, ever-increasing individual, lower-level night missions—all with tremendous success.

With the complete destruction or total surrender of the Japanese Empire in sight, night missions fell into a well-planned pattern. Send out two or three B-29 Pathfinders each trio to dozens of widely separated targets, in advance of hundreds of individual, single-plane take-offs, at staggered intervals (for safety) throughout the night. The Pathfinders pinpointed their individual targets, usually a city with military potential, by dropping a string of incendiaries in-trail (one after the other in a line) at the left perimeter of the targeted city, preferably the up-wind edge, and the second Pathfinder dropped a string along the right edge of the target. The third dropped its line of fire between the other two.

The first arriving B-29 (at the highest altitude) dropped between two lines of making fire. The subsequent arrivals, at slightly lower altitudes each time, bisected lines of fire until there was total conflagration, sometimes even greater than 100% of the denoted target area, depending on which direction the fire was carried by surface winds.

No matter how they were flown—day, night, en mass, or individually—they were long tiring, over hundreds of miles of open sea, physically exhausting, mentally numbing, tortuous missions, for the most part, unbelievably boring, and absolutely necessary.

In Korea, it was a two-man crew flying solo missions aboard B-26Cs in the dead of night on low-level seek and destroy interdiction strikes through the deep, narrow canyons of Korea's rugged mountains. It was split-second, wild, seat-of-your-pants flying. Streaking out of the night sky, down through narrow canyons, lighting up the railways and valley roads with napalm from wing pods—1500 pounds of fifty-caliber ammo in the wings and mixed loads of incendiary, armor piercing, and anti-personnel bombs in the bays.

As it turned out, Harry Spillers was one of the best, if not the best, combat pilot in the whole outfit. He was a natural. He flew the B-26C as if he was part of it. Harry and I started flying missions together and got in seven in the first eleven nights, developing our own attack routine as we went along. We fine-tuned it with each mission until it became formulaic. Find and identify the first target in our area of interdiction, line up parallel to the course established by the target.

All roads and railways in the mountainous regions of North Korea follow the base of the mountains, usually adjacent to the path of creek or river, which almost guaranteed that our attack would be in line with a valley or a divide between two mountain ranges. We always ran the southern boundary of our assigned area first, so that anything coming toward our position would be traveling south. This assured us a frontal attack on any southbound convoy loaded with ammunition or reinforcement personnel. We maneuvered, at a safe altitude, to line up with the target, open the bomb bay doors, activate the arming switches, and started gliding; throttle back to reduce engine noise so as not to alert our quarry. As the first lights in the convoy passed under our nose, I would call, "Okay, Harry, drop the nose." By waiting until that moment, where the nose abruptly came down, the lights of the first truck in the convoy was in his sights.

We used this attack whether bombing or strafing. We had found the bombsight to be useless in this type of fighting. This way, we used the airplane as the point of attack—no concern for altitude, trail, or wind corrections. We eliminated altitude in the dive. Without altitude, there was very little trail effect, and the bombs were in the air for such a short time, wind direction meant almost nothing; we had eliminated the bugs inherent in precision bombing, except speed. We didn't want the air speed constant—the faster the better. We were combining dive and skip bombing.

I called for "pull out," and as the nose started up, punched out a string of bombs in trail—one after another in a sequence. We always got rid of the bombs first to lighten our weight and increase maneuverability. The number of bombs and timing of each release was determined by the length and number of vehicles in the convoy being attacked.

Our initial goal was to stop the convoy; hence, the attack on the lead vehicle. The next objective was destruction and fire, which gave us illumination for subsequent attacks. If we had been carrying napalm on our exterior wing-pods, they would have gone first, to reduce drag and weight and guarantee illumination. After the initial attack, we were often confronted with anti-aircraft crossfire in our line of attack from opposing emplacements on elevated positions on two parallel mountain ranges. If I was able to spot their approximate positions, they became our next targets.

At the end of the bombing or strafing run, we would climb above the mountain peaks, make a tight turn, then dive down again from the opposite direction and resume the attack from the rear. The same climb, turn, and dive would continue throughout the night on various targets of opportunity, until we had exhausted our armament and headed home.

Harry and I made for a great team. We did our best to perform our mission each night with confidence and integrity. The missions were, for the most part, unsupervised, highly specialized, individual challenges of ability and honor. No one was looking over your shoulder; you were on your own. It was your pride, your honor, your honesty—your job.

On this particular night, I was to ride as crew with a dumb-ass cowboy named Major Beauregard, squadron exec of another flight. It was the brilliant idea of pencil-pushing desk jockeys at headquarters to rotate flight personnel and insure that seldom-flying squadron geeks got their combat hours in to qualify for another ribbon, pin, or rate to hang on the front of their class A's.

Major Beauregard was a demented, sadistic, completely self-centered egomaniac. The hair on the back of my neck stood on end when I saw him swagger onto the flight line with his ten-gallon head, ten-gallon belt buckle, ten-gallon boots, and bullshit pearl-handled revolver. The field grade nincompoop did everything possible to tear the wings off and heart out of a damn fine airplane.

We were tooling along at about 8,000 feet. The night was dark and weather calm when the nose lurched upward, pinning me to the floor (no restraints in the nose). The plane wheeled onto its left wing and plunged straight toward the ground, screaming like a wounded animal. I was smashed to the over-head Plexiglas by the sudden G-forces and could do nothing but hang in there and watch, completely helpless. I had seen noth-ing, and still hadn't seen anything, when the 50s came clattering out of the forward guns. Incendiaries, spaced about twenty rounds apart, lit a trail to the ground, and I still couldn't spot the target.

With the incendiaries spotting the way, I guess he could see we were getting pretty close to the ground. He pulled up and climbed out of there, of course; with reversing G forces, I was slammed face-first into the bombsite and remained glued to the deck until we leveled out at about 6,000 feet. Not a word had been said over the intercom—no communication whatsoever. Asshole.

We swung back and forth across the width of our assigned area, wasting fuel and finding nothing. I spotted what could have been one or two vehicles, or a couple of guys lighting cigarettes, and decided to keep my eye on the area for a bit and see what developed. All of a sudden, the nose dropped out from under me again. I was again slammed to the overhead on my back, and down we went in a hell-bent screaming dive. Quasi-modo had apparently spotted the tiny flicker of light out of the corner of his eye and taken the plunge.

The 50s came crashing out again, not in short, well-aimed bursts, but in seemingly unending streams. About halfway down, the fifties started cooking off as they emerged from the overheated barrels. The incendiary rounds exploded in a flash of bright white lights just forward of the wing's leading edge. Flash blindness and loss of night vision results in a split-second. He froze; he stayed in the screaming dive, fifties still exploding in blinding white flashes.

"Pull up! Pull up!" I yelled. "You're going to smash us into the mountain!"

I bolted upright, covered in clammy sweat. I didn't know if I had woken myself when I yelled. I was breathing heavy, and my pulse was racing; there was dead silence. Suddenly, I hard the creaking step in the stairwell at the end of the hall. I felt my damp shirt and realized I hadn't undressed when I came in; I had just thrown my jacket on the chair and flopped down across the bed.

I listened carefully, and there came a creak in the floorboard as someone approached down the darkened hall. I quietly slid to the floor between the bed and the wall. I placed the pillow lengthwise in the middle of the bed and pulled the cover over it. I lay on the floor under the bed and waited. I slid my .38 from beneath my arm and watched under the door as someone's shadow stopped in front of it. The doorknob turned slowly. It was locked. I heard the telltale scratching as he jimmied the lock. Again, the doorknob turned, and the shadowy figure slowly opened the door. Just a crack at first, then he opened the door and quietly stepped in.

Two quick muzzle flashes lit the room like a strobe, punctu-ating the chunk-chunk sound of the silencer. The room filled with acrid blue smoke and the smell of spent gunpowder.

He fired once more before I put two bullets into his torso. He flew backward in the air and slammed into the wall across the hallway, then slumped to the floor. My ears were ringing from the close-quarter fire of my .38, and I was blinded by the muzzle-flashes and thick smoke. To my amazement, I heard him struggle to his feet and scramble down the hall to the stairwell. Before I could pull myself from under the bed, he had stumbled down the stairs and out the front door.

I ran down the hall and leaped the stairs to the landing below. I crouched down, opened the door, and looked out in time to see him run across the courtyard and disappear around the building next door, uphill, away from the harbor. I ran across the courtyard and stopped at the corner of the building. I looked around the corner and saw him run up the hill then turn down an alley, back toward town. I followed him up the street to the alley and slowly peered around the corner of the building. A crashing blow exploded between my eyes and knocked me sprawling to the ground. A warm whooshing sound swallowed even the ringing in my ears. Sparks whirled through darkened vision.

Black and white, silent, and in slow motion, he stepped out from the alley. The lone streetlight behind him gave his ominous and deliberate movement a nightmarish silhouette. The Grim Reaper incarnate. The glint of light reflected off the blue steel muzzle through the haze, as my .38 rose from the ground and fired two more times, hitting him squarely in the chest, hurling him backward, and thumping him to the ground like a silent sack of potatoes.

I slowly pulled myself up. The sparkles were beginning to clear, and the whooshing sound was fading, only to be replaced by the ringing in my ears. Function began to return to real time, normal speed. I slowly staggered to where my assailant lay sprawled on the pavement. I wiped the blood beginning to stream from the bridge of my nose with the back of my hand. I couldn't believe this guy had gotten up and run all this way after I put two slugs in him back at the boarding house. His lungs should have been blown out of the gaping hole the hollow points should have created in his back.

As I approached he suddenly kicked out with his leg, sweeping my feet out from under me, sending me crashing to the ground. Before I knew it, he was up on his feet and running back into the alley. He fired two more shots as he disappeared into the darkness. The first shot struck the pavement directly in front of me, pelting me with bits of asphalt as the slug zinged off the street, zipped past my head, and imbedded itself in the side of a house across the way. The second sent shards of hot shrapnel and bits of cement to pepper the car parked at the curb.

I got to my feet and ran into the alley after him. I heard him blindly crashing into metal trashcans that lined both sides of the narrowing dark path behind the adjacent homes. The alley began to descend the hill at an increasingly steep slope. We reached a point at which there were no longer any buildings lining the narrow path; instead, thick, sharp pampas grass grew tall overhead on both sides.

I could no longer see him or his silhouette. Nor could I hear him running down the steep pavement. I ran blindly into the darkness of what seemed to be a narrowing tunnel. I was Alice chasing the rabbit into Wonderland. I should have known better.

Suddenly, a blow exploded at the back of my skull, sending me tumbling head over heels down the embankment and into the pampas grass. I scrambled to my hands and knees just in time to stare into the business end of a blue steel silencer screwed onto the front of a big, ugly .45 auto. He had me. I was dead meat.

Then, out of nowhere, something that sounded like a hummingbird zinged past my head. The guy holding the .45 in front of me grabbed the side of his neck and looked at me with astonishment etched grotesquely into his face. Long streams of blood began to squirt out from between his fingers in pulsating currents. His face turned ashen, and then he simply keeled over, landing heavily, flat on his back.

The stream of blood gushing from his neck gradually got smaller and smaller until, with the final beats of his heart, it diminished to a trickle that led to a pool around him as he lay lifeless on the pavement.

I heard sirens approaching and saw the flashing lights dance across the hillsides as squad cars screeched to a stop at both ends of the narrow path. Within seconds, the area was swarming with cops, flashlights, and guns. I was dazed, stunned. I felt the gash between my eyes and the small mouse that was beginning to form under it. My ears continued to ring, and the stars swirling about my brain made it difficult for me to get up to speed or comprehend what had just occurred. Time and space blurred. I could not re-focus. I felt the back of my skull and came upon a growing egg and the sticky seepage of my own warm blood.

It was the twilight, just before sunrise, when Inspector La-Farge arrived on the scene. I heard the sound of his jack-boots stomping hard upon the paved incline as he approached. He barked a few terse orders to his men and came straight over to where I sat nursing my lumpy cranium.

"I knew it!" he said angrily. "I just knew I would find you right in the middle of all this as soon as I heard the call," yelled the inspector. "Goddamn you, Dugan, you son of a bitch, I told you to keep your goddamn weapon in your pants while you were here. I knew I would wind up with a growing pile of mangled bodies as soon as you got involved. What in the hell is your problem, anyway?"

"Well," I began. "I've got a couple of lumps on my noggin', and I think I've torn my new trousers. Nothing, really, but thank you for asking."

He apparently failed to see the humor in my facetiousness. Jocularity was obviously not what the annoyed inspector had on his mind the first thing this morning. He ripped into a heated tirade rifled with expletives that would make a longshoreman blush. His tantrum continued until he brought it to a dramatic crescendo by slamming his cap to the ground and angrily kicking it across the road. I got the impression that he was not a happy constable.

"Jeeze," I finally said playfully. "Don't get your pantaloons in a pucker, Frenchy. I didn't kill the guy. I'm the victim here."

"Some victim," he shot back angrily. "This guy's lying in a pool of his own blood, and your worst complaint is that you scuffed your goddamn shoes?"

By this time, the medical examiner had arrived. He kneeled beside the body and removed something from the neck wound. He examined it then brought it to Constable LaFarge.

It was a round metal object about the size of a silver dollar, ringed around the outside edge by a series of sharp points, with a hole through the middle. It looked similar to a Star of David medallion. It wasn't. I knew exactly what it was.

Inspector LaFarge wiped off the object then brought it to me.

"Do you know what this is?" he asked.

"Yes, it's a Chinese star dart," I answered. He paused, waiting for me to explain.

I had no explanation. I told him how the thing came whizzing by me from behind and hit the guy's neck. I never saw who threw it. Whoever it was, he damn sure knew how to use it. With the amount of blood, and the way the geyser spurted from his neck, it had obviously punctured the jugular.

Inspector LaFarge continued to fidget with the shiny implement and stared intently into my eyes when the medical examiner called him over to the body. After conferring with the coroner for a moment, the inspector motioned me over. I got to my feet with some difficulty and walked over to the corpse. Now I knew how he continued to function after I put four slugs into him. He was wearing a vest. It was a thick, crude heavy vest like a guy in the military would wear to diffuse a bomb or dig up a land mine. It looked cumbersome, but it sure did the job. Too bad it wasn't a turtleneck version.

The medical examiner probed the holes my .38 had created in the vest through layers of heavy woven fabric and corrugated material that looked like a fiberboard of some kind. He eventually came up with a slightly distorted hollow point slug. My persuader had knocked the hell out of the guy, but hadn't penetrated the vest. It made me begin to re-evaluate the whole snub nose .38 concept.

The snubby was good at short distances or in close quarters, where I do most of my work. It's an urban weapon. It blasts big holes in victims, but errant shots don't travel too far and hit innocent bystanders. It packs enough punch to knock the hell out of an assailant, and the short barrel produces an explosion that gets everybody's attention. But I have had a .38 slug bounce off a windshield without penetrating, and had great big guys seemingly not affected by several slugs pumped into them and continue to advance—for a short distance, anyway. A .38 was small and compact, easy to conceal, and it packed a good wallop at close range. But in some instances, it wasn't enough firepower, and it was virtually useless at long range.

The inspector asked me if I recognized the guy. I didn't. Then he searched the guy's pockets. He retrieved a couple hundred in chump change and a room key from the Atwater Hotel. He carried no wallet or ID. Next, the inspector rifled around in the lining of the guy's clothes. All tags had been removed. The good inspector was a professional. He was well versed in the sequence of investigative events and techniques. It was reassuring to know that he knew what he was doing.

Constable LaFarge had cordoned off the area and instructed his men to conduct a thorough search for evidence, such as spent shell casings and items dropped in the chase. He also dispatched a contingent of officers to the end of the alley and Mrs. O'Malley's boarding house.

After a terse investigation, the inspector announced the obvious. The guy was a professional hit man sent to whack yours truly. As if the silencer and bulletproof vest weren't a dead give away. No pun intended.

Finally, he gave me back my piece and sent me on my way—with another stern warning, of course. He instructed me to check in at the end of the day and he would inform me what, if anything, he turned up on my would-be assassin. I apologized for the inconvenience and mess. Why I was apologizing, I had no idea. I headed back up the steep path towards Mrs. O'Malley's.

Chapter 11

A Smorgasbord of Delights and Other Noontime Treats

I reached the boarding house just as LaFarge's men were leaving. Leaving a hell of a mess, if I knew my police searches.

Mrs. O'Malley met me at the door and escorted me to the service porch, where she began to tend to my head wounds. She cleaned up the cut between my eyes and gave me an ice pack for the swelling. Before sending me to my room, she informed me that the inspector's men had thoroughly searched it, but had left it, for the most part, the way they had found it. She assured me that she had watched them closely, and thought that they had not removed anything.

"I'm sorry for the trouble, Mrs. O'Malley," I said. "I didn't intend to bring any problems to your home."

"Now don't you worry about that, son," she said in her enchanting Irish brogue. "I used to run a speak-easy downstairs—you know, during prohibition—and a home for wayward women upstairs, if you know what I mean. So don't you concern yourself with me, son, 'cause I've seen it all. And besides," she said with a big grin, "you've got a fine Irish name and an honest face, my boy. I'm honored to know you. Now you go and get yourself cleaned up, and I'll go see if I can find some decent clothes for you to wear. I'm sure I've got something that will do."

Before she went about her task, she stopped and whispered, "Oh, by the by, son, there was a giant mountain of a Chinaman hangin' around just before the police arrived. He was actin' as if he was going to come in, but I kept my eye on him through the window, and he never did. Then the constable's men arrived, and he quickly left. Oh, I almost forgot. The policemen did remove three slugs from your mattress, but I'm quite sure that's all they took." She patted me on the cheek and went to find clothes.

I went to my room, searched my jacket pockets, and came up with the inventory list and ring of keys that Harry Peters had given me yesterday. I looked through the list and sure enough, there on the last page, typed in with a different script than the rest, was what I was looking for. Someone, I assume Harry Peters, had typed onto the bottom of the list, "Statuette/gold paint over lead/ dragon/ Chinese/ red and green stones." And just below that was the entry, "Seal/ bronze/ Chinese inscription."

I cleaned up as quickly as I could, splashed on some froufrou water, and got myself downtown. Mrs. O'Malley had supplied me with a nifty beige sports jacket and trousers. She even came up with a nearly new shirt, socks, and a very nice pair of brown loafers, including tassels. I was pretty spiffy when I breezed into town searching for a cup of coffee and an aspirin. I went to the Pancake House on the corner of Crescent and Metropole and ordered a bagel, coffee and a couple of aspirin.

I perused my inventory lists while I ate. There was nothing out of the ordinary that I could see, other than the two items added to the bottom of the last page. If I was correct in my assumption that Harry Peters had added the two items, he must have intimate knowledge regarding their whereabouts. How could this myopic little toad-faced crud possibly know about the Kubla Khan treasure? Or suspect they were on the island? Could either of the mysterious consorts that have already sought me out have approached him? Or did he have information from other sources? Why would a demure, slightly neurotic, diminutive corporate accountant be privy to secret information about lost treasure? And what the hell business was it of his, anyway?

I finished my breakfast, such as it was, and went looking for a telephone before heading off to the casino. I hoped that Precious could provide some answers. I was getting antsy about the progress of the investigation. I needed to get up to speed.

I went back down the street toward the harbor and stopped at a cluster of heavy, wooden phone booths across from the tourist information center. I was feeling surprisingly chipper, considering my alcohol intake last night and the two rousing thumps to the fore and aft of my cranium this morning. The swelling between my eyes had subsided considerably, and the cut was not nearly as horrendous as all the blood had suggested. Head wounds always bled profusely and appeared much more serious than they turned out to be—if you're lucky. Once you clean them up, the actual wound may be no more than a shaving nick. The lump on the back of my head was still a nice little egg, however.

I dropped a dime in the slot and gave the operator the number. I followed that with a king's ransom worth of coins and lit a cigarette while waiting for the connection. After a dazzling series of clicks, pops, and a variety of fuzz and buzzes came the familiar voice of Precious Goodlay. "Good morning, Travis Dugan Private Investigations," she said.

"Top o' the mornin', gorgeous! How is my precious Precious this fine morning?"

"For God's sake," she responded. "You really have been full of stuff and vinegar since you got there, haven't you, Travis? What is it? The sea air? The water? Or the margaritas that give you that bushy tail first thing in the morning? Or perhaps it's some bushy tail named Margarita, no?"

I had to laugh. For being such a classy dame, Precious could really be pretty crude. She had the vocabulary of a drunken sailor.

"So, my dear," I said. "Have you done your homework and come up with any useful information regarding the three gentlemen of which we spoke?"

"Yes, I have that information right here. These are some interesting characters you've come up with, Trav. They're from rather diverse backgrounds—the far-flung corners of the world. I had to pull out all the stops to get a line on these guys.

"Your Chief Constable LaFarge is French Algerian," she began. "He seems to be living out of a suitcase lately. He recently traveled from Algiers to Morocco, then Morocco to Martinique, in the Caribbean. From Martinique to Havana to Miami; Miami to Avalon. All within the last couple of years. He comes with impeccable credentials and an impressive law enforcement background, but he seems to be on some kind of quest lately. The good inspector is either following or running from something or someone.

"The next one is quite a character," she continued. "I'll bet you have no idea who Sir Arthur Sydney is, do you?"

"Well, he claims to be a world-traveling art connoisseur with dubious connections to the British government," I responded.

"Yes, that is true. He is indeed what he says he is. But he's much more intriguing than that," she continued with obvious interest. "You see, while his title may be purchased, his grandfather indeed had knighthood bestowed upon him. His grandfather is the founder and publisher of Ganeway's *Guide to Military Aircraft, Ships, and Ground-Force Armaments and Weaponry*, considered the Bible of weapons and ordinance capabilities, used by virtually every intelligence agency in the free world. Sir Arthur's family is very elite, with ties to British intelligence. They are rumored to be involved in the most delicate covert operations involving national security and operations with global ramifications. This is an illustrious family with a lot of juice and lots of insulation. Very deep cover. You're lucky I have the connections I have, or you wouldn't be getting any of this information. It is all very hush-hush off the cuff stuff.

"Be careful, Travis. From what I gather, Sir Arthur is heavily involved with numerous international conspiracies, and not averse to assisting interests other than those of the British government. While he is indeed an art connoisseur and dealer of some renown and respect within such circles, I believe those endeavors are merely a cover for intelligence gathering and other sinister enterprises, including black market arms sales— and I'm not talkin' slingshots and switchblades, Travis. I'm talkin' state of the art ballistic missiles and weapons systems— very sophisticated weaponry. Does that spin your propeller, or what? The man is a provocateur and a privateer," she warned. "And he knows his way around. He may seem harmless and jovial, but he is cunning, devious, and cruel. Be very careful around him, Travis. Stay on your toes. Don't get lulled into complacency. He is a very sinister and dangerous fellow. He's a cunning shark in a murky sea. A piranha in a guppy pond. Last, but certainly not least on your list is the enigmatic, elusive Nicky Fallon."

"Huh? Elusive? Enigmatic?"

"Yes," she responded. "Young Nicky Fallon has apparently gone to some length to conceal his true identity. He had no past until he entered Harvard about six years ago. He graduated magna cum laude with a degree in corporate law. What do you think about that?"

Silence.

"Immediately upon graduation, he went to work for some of the finest casinos in Havana and Miami. Has some very good connections, doesn't he?"

More silence.

"Miami is where he met Johnny Rigney. He eventually came to work for him in the casino in Avalon. Was that an interesting, unrelated set of circumstances, or a carefully planned chain of events? Huh? What do you think, Travis? What's up with that?"

Still more silence.

"Well, that's all I have for you today, stud."

"Wait," I said. Her guppy pond analogy had gotten me to thinking. "What do you know about a Limey named Blaine Pond? Thirtyish, dashing, handsome, well educated, very articulate. He claims to be a representative of some outfit called the East-Asian Trading Company."

"Ahha!" she laughed. "Well I can tell you straightaway that the East-Asian Trading Company, while a thriving international import and export enterprise, was originally established as a front for British intelligence operating out of the Crown's colony in Hong Kong and Singapore. If Mr. Pond is indeed with the East-Asian Trading Company, then you can bet your crumpets that he is a British agent. And furthermore," she said, "if British intelligence is on the island and Sir Arthur Sidney is on the island as well, then a fortune in lost treasure is at stake. For God's sake, be careful, Travis."

She was right. I was in way over my head, but there was no turning back now. I was in for the duration. "Okay, Precious, I've got two more names for you. The first is a Chinaman named Que Kane Chang. He's in his fifties, five-eight, hundred and eighty pounds. Says he represents the Nationalist Government of China. He and a smarmy little Tong named Ahn Hai are looking for items presumed to be from the lost treasure of Kubla Khan. He seems to think that P.K. Rigney recovered some the treasure in the East China Sea and somehow secreted a jewel-encrusted dragon and bronze seal back to the island. The fat man, Sir Arthur, confirms just such a possibility and says he is likewise interested in those specific items.

"The second man is also Chinese," I continue. "The only name I have come up with is Doctor Con. He's small—about five-foot-five, maybe a hundred and fifty pounds. He operates a bat guano mine, of all things, on the windward side of the island. Apparently, his operations don't sit well with the city counsel or the island's Conservancy Committee. I'm afraid that's about all I know about him, except that Blaine Pond is hot on his trail. There must be something afoot there. See what you can dig up for me will you, Precious? I'll call you again tomorrow morning."

I dropped another numismatic symbol of debt into the slot and spun the dial. Rita Rigney answered the phone. I confirmed our luncheon appointment for this afternoon, and asked about the other family members' schedules for today. I was not entirely surprised to learn that Lara was indeed meeting Blaine Pond at noon for a tour of the ceramics factory on the island.

I didn't much like the idea of her spending the afternoon in the company of the dashing British agent, but at least she would be in capable hands. Maybe that's what worried me. I said goodbye to my luscious luncheon partner and headed toward the casino.

I arrived at the office normally occupied by Harry the toad boy. One of the sextuplet secretaries informed me that Mr. Peters had gone to the bird sanctuary to view any objects d'art or treasure that might belong to the inventory of his on-going audit.

I felt uneasy about Harry searching the treasure vault unattended. I was torn between hustling over there to keep an eye on him and staying here, making a feeble attempt to find some of the items on my list. I reluctantly decided to leave Harry to his own devices for now and doggedly pursue my duties as paleontologist, archaeologist, underpaid, under-qualified warehouseman.

I found a pair of coveralls in a janitorial closet, made my way up to the attic, and began to catalog the items on my list. It was dusty, tedious work, but it gave me an opportunity to see just what secrets the attic contained.

The attic mostly contained filing cabinets full of old documents, building plans, and spec sheets having to do with the original construction of the casino. Other files contained agreements, covenants, conditions, restrictions, and contacts with such entities as the Catalina Cattle Company, the Catalina steamer, and other mining and fishing rights contacts. The contents of the various files were old and yellowed.

One cabinet contained documents and agreements with the defense department. These documents dealt with billeting arrangements for military personnel on an area of the island now inhabited by Cooley Town. Other documents included mooring rights for naval vessels conducting artillery and bombing exercises around the neighboring island of San Clemente. San Clemente Island was an uninhabited island southwest of Catalina. It was used exclusively by the military to conduct amphibious assaults, naval artillery practice, and aircraft bombing and strafing runs. San Clemente was off limits to all but defense department military personnel and equipment.

The documents seemed to indicate that the navy utilized mooring facilities in an area known as White's Landing, now used by the commercial fishing fleet, and billeted military personnel in a camp of bungalows now inhabited by the Chinese immigrants.

Throughout the morning, I managed to find many of the items on my list. There was nothing unique on the list or in the attic. I was rather disappointed. I was hoping to find something to point me in the right direction. The smoking gun. The key that unlocks the case. Having concluded that I had found all there was to be found, I locked the door and headed to the dungeon that was the basement.

I spent the remainder of the morning searching through haphazard piles of furniture, assembled and disassembled, discarded paintings, dusty statuary, décor items, and display cases. Again, I managed to actually find several of the items contained in my inventory list, conducted a thorough search of the basement, and had a pretty good grasp of what was contained within the basement walls that seemed now, to be closing in on me. I got the uneasy feeling that this chore was designed to keep me out of the way. I needed to get out of here.

I closed the basement door and locked it behind me. I returned the coveralls to the janitorial closet and washed up in the employees' restroom adjacent to the offices. I exited the casino by way of the employees' ramp and walked the short distance along the harbor to the yacht club, which was perched atop sturdy pilings over the water next to the steamship pier.

It was a bright, beautiful afternoon, so I opted for an umbrella table on the open deck overlooking the harbor. The premiere of the three-night International Film Festival was to take place this evening and many celebrities had begun arriving this morning. The harbor was filled with expensive pleasure boats, and the restaurant was crowded with tanned movie people—babes.

I ordered a bloody mary from a preppie cabin boy and enjoyed the warm sunshine, anticipating the arrival of my vivacious luncheon partner. I didn't have to wait long. My pulse quickened when I spotted Rita coming down the boardwalk. She was a stunning love child. Her walk was free-spirited and bouncy. As was the entire package. Bouncy, perky, and exciting. She wore a tight knit top, white with horizontal black stripes stretched to distortion. Her taut breasts strained against the thin material, and her nipples danced the dance of firm youth. She wore white shorts, white deck shoes, and a matching white sailor cap. Her long dark hair and dark skin vibrantly contrasted the bright nautical outfit.

Upon her arrival at the table, she gave me a quick kiss and a spirited caress of my thigh. My enthusiasm was obvious. Her smile was inspiring. Her caress lingered, and my leg began to quiver with anticipation. She could have put a leash on me and led me away like an obedient lamb to the slaughter.

"Well, I see both of you are of one mind," she said teasingly. "I hope I can live up to your expectations."

The cabin boy appeared again, and she ordered a strawberry margarita while we perused the menu. Rita ordered crab salad, and anything was fine with me at this point, as long as it didn't take too long to prepare.

We engaged in intimate conversation sprinkled with sexual innuendo while waiting for the crab salad. I could hardly contain my exuberance, and the glass tabletop provided very little in the way of camouflage.

Our lunch finally arrived. I gobbled ravenously. She gently placed her hand on my thigh and said, "Calm down, boys, we have all afternoon. Don't be in such a hurry. Take your time. Enjoy yourselves."

For dessert, Rita ordered strawberries and whipped cream. I had the time of my life just watching her. She would dip the strawberry into the whipped cream then lick just a little off with the very end of her talented tongue. When all the cream had been removed from the fruit, she would then gently place it between her lips and softly caress it. I never enjoyed dessert quite so much before without ever having taken even one bite.

We finished our lunch and began walking along the harbor back toward town and the mansion. I had no idea where we were going, but Rita seemed to have a place in mind, so I followed like a lovesick puppy. We walked south along the water's edge and eventually came to the private mooring of R.J.'s boat, *The Lucky Dutchman*.

The Lucky Dutchman was a sleek, finely appointed converted Navy sub-chaser. Her twin diesels and props made for lightning speed through the water; it was a highly maneuverable, yet extremely stable ride. It was a fine craft.

Rita turned the key in the lock and we entered a luxurious stateroom. The enormous lounge was posh and elegantly appointed with the same black walnut woodwork found in the casino. She moved behind the bar and removed her sailor's cap and knit top. She poured two brandies and came out from behind the bar sans her little white shorts, as well. We toasted to an enchanting afternoon, then she took me by the hand and led me to the captain's cabin, where a large expanse of plush bed awaited.

We spent the afternoon indulging ourselves in unadulterated, lustful exuberance, pausing only occasionally for rest and refreshment. During one such respite, she lit us both a cigarette. I said that I was unaware that she smoked. "I only smoke after sex," she answered with a devilish grin. "I'm up to half a pack a day."

Ya gotta love this girl. And I did—over and over again.

Rita Rigney was exotically sexy, fun, and uninhibited. She was also young and rich—everything I desired in a woman. For the remainder of the afternoon, Rita and I blissfully danced across the pages of my carnal repertoire, occasionally repeating some of the more challenging passages. I was a concert conductor, expertly handling my magic wand, orchestrating a sexathon concerto to standing ovations and multiple encores. Once we had exhausted my catalog of erotic sonnets, we began to delve into her imaginative menu of libidinous fantasies.

Hers was an Olympic-caliber gymnastics exhibition. Her performance included vaults, handsprings, somersaults, and demonstrations of strength and flexibility. It was a flawless performance, culminating with an intricate and highly dangerous dismount. (Kids, do not try this at home.) She was judged on degree of difficulty and presentation of routine. She did very well in the compulsories and was magnificent in the free-style program. I gave her a perfect ten. It was indeed a gold medal performance.

By the time we awakened from exhausted sleep, it was approaching the end of the day and a luminous scarlet sunset awaited us.

While we showered, she became aware and mentioned in passing, her observation of the wondrous capabilities of the prehensile male member and its predisposition to react with a mind of its own. She concluded her astute observation by stating that it is probably why some men are commonly referred to as pecker heads. As I said before, you gotta love this girl—over and over.

Chapter 12

The Premier

Rita and I arrived back at the mansion just after sunset and just prior to Lara Rigney's return from her factory tour with Blaine Pond. Upon entering the foyer, Rita bid me adieu and went to her room to prepare for the evening's festivities. Before she exited, I thanked her again for the glorious afternoon. She blew me a kiss from afar and ascended the staircase upon which I had first laid eyes upon her. I watched as she climbed the stairs and disappeared from view. I smiled and turned to go, whereupon I was once again brought up short by a disapproving Spaulding—the family butler and resident pain in the neck.

"Damn you, Spaulding. Didn't I tell you before not to sneak up on me like that?"

"Terribly sorry, sir," he said. "I wasn't aware that someone could sneak up on such a finely honed specimen of personal protection as yourself." (Spaulding—what a zero.) "I assure you," he continued, "I certainly had no such intention, sir. Perhaps you were momentarily distracted by something?" he asked innocently, with his infamous raised brow of disgust.

"Yes, perhaps I was," I said, glancing up at the now-empty staircase. "What's on your mind, Spaulding?"

"Mr. Rigney would like to have a word with you out on the terrace. You may find your own way, sir. I thought perhaps I might lay out an appropriate wardrobe for this evening for you, sir. If you don't mind?"

"Thank you, Spaulding. That's very thoughtful of you. That would be fine."

I found the Commodore in his usual spot, sipping brandy and enjoying a fine Havana.

"Good evening, Commodore," I said upon my arrival. "It's a glorious sunset, isn't it?"

"Ah, Mr. Dugan, so very glad to see you, sir. Please, have a seat; pour yourself a brandy, and help yourself to a cigar. I'm very pleased to see you. I trust all is going well? And yes, that is a very glorious sunset, indeed."

The Commodore seemed to be in good spirits this evening.

"You know, Mr. Dugan," he began. "My favorite times of day are sunrise and sunset. Sunrise, of course, because it means I've made it one more day. But beyond the obvious, sunrise is so pristine and somehow mystical. The warm sunlight and gossamer morning haze rising from the calm, pale water. I realize it sounds silly, but sunrise makes me feel rather Hobbit-like. Ahhh! Ahhh! Do you think me a silly old man who's beginning to lose touch with reality, Mr. Dugan? Or do you think I'm a lonely old bastard who's killing time by pulling your leg?"

"No, no," I responded. "I agree wholeheartedly. A good, pristine sunrise always make same feel rather Hobbit-like, too."

"Ahhh! Mr. Dugan, you are indeed full of the blarney," he said. "And I commend you for it, sir. I thank you for your well-humored indulgence as well."

"And the sunsets, Commodore?"

"Ah, yes, the sunsets," he lamented. "So serene, so exquisitely peaceful and romantic. Those are the moments when an old man such as myself reflects on times gone by. Loves won and lost. The accomplishments in one's life, and yes, the regrets, too. Those are the times I find it warm and comforting— reminiscent of days gone by. It is also a time of sorrow and loneliness. If I may plagiarize Mr. Dickens—'It was the best of times, it was the worst of times.'"

We sat quietly for a while, sipping brandy and smoking Havanas. Together, we sat and gazed at the radiant sunset and enjoyed the warmth of the gentle Santa Ana breezes. Santa Anas are warm desert winds that blow offshore from the mainland during the summer, bringing warm temperatures to the beaches and island, as opposed to the cool on-shore breezes that come from the sea.

Another feature of the Santa Anas is that with the warm inland winds come the fine dust particles and a certain amount of pollutants that make for gloriously beautiful sunsets to the west. To the north, in the Santa Barbara area, these same winds are called "sundowners."

After the orange and red ball of the sun slipped below the dark horizon of smooth ocean, the Commodore set his glass down and asked how my investigation was progressing. I took my time and slowly filled him in on all that had occurred to this point. He listened quietly, thoughtfully. I asked if he knew anything about the Kubla Khan treasure, and if P.K. actually had managed to secret items from that expedition back to the island.

The old man sat in quiet contemplation for a short while. Then he spoke softly and deliberately. He explained that if P.K. had indeed managed to transfer items from such a highly sought-after treasure, he certainly would not have said items delivered to Sumner Renton or anyone connected with the museum. Furthermore, with the apparent danger associated with such articles, he likewise would not have had the items arrive at the mansion. Because of the absolute secrecy and trust required, the only person P.K. could have ultimately entrusted with such responsibility would have been his brother Johnny. He further theorized that if such were indeed the case, Johnny's disappearance most certainly would be connected to the treasure.

I assured the Commodore that I was investigating leads with that possibility in mind, which brought me to the question of the identities of Nicky Fallon and Sir Arthur Sydney.

He explained that Johnny had taken over the day-to-day operations of the casino and ballroom several years ago, and had not only tightened up the organization from top to bottom, but had also returned the casino to the pre-eminence of its heyday, during Prohibition. He would certainly have investigated Mr. Fallon's background thoroughly prior to his employment.

As for Sir Arthur Sydney, the Commodore was not familiar with the gentleman except for vague recollections of a connection to the family that published a weapons catalog of some sort.

I complimented the Commodore on his cognitive resources and filled in the details as I knew them. Though he found the mystique fascinating, he could not be of further help. He was not aware of any secret treasure arriving on the island, but he felt as I did—it was certainly worth looking into.

It was about this time that Lara Rigney arrived back at the mansion after her afternoon in the company of Blaine Pond. In the warm sunset, she looked positively radiant—at least, I hoped that's why she looked radiant.

She breezed in, pink-cheeked, wind-blown, and glowing. The hair on the back of my neck began to stand on end. After the day I'd had with her precocious sister, I still felt jealous about Lara and her Limey playboy. She kissed the old man on the cheek and excitedly told him about her day at the ceramics factory. Spaulding finally arrived to escort the Commodore to the dining room for his supper.

I asked a few innocuous questions about her afternoon. She blew me a kiss on the run and said she would tell me all about it tonight at the film festival. With that, she disappeared upstairs to prepare for this evening's premier. Before adjourning to my room, I checked on the security arrangements for this evening and house staff and family's agendas. Having completed my rounds, I retired to my quarters to prepare for tonight's gala social fest.

As usual, we had Roscoe retrieve Mrs. Rigney and myself from the estate and deliver us to the casino. Once again, the entire area was aglow with searchlights crisscrossing the night sky and throngs of elegant and excited participants.

Tonight, the opening night of the three-day film festival, featured a Demille Hollywood Biblical extravaganza. Big stars, big scenes, big budget. And Hollywood turned out in droves, dressed to the nines. The film festival exuded the glamour and excess associated with a big Hollywood premier. And because this was an international film festival, producers, directors, and stars from around the world turned out for the party.

Tonight's activities included the opening night premier, followed by dinner and dancing in the ballroom. Tomorrow and tomorrow night would be exclusively foreign films, and the third and final night of the festival would close with a Busby Berkley romantic musical-comedy spectacular.

Roscoe delivered Mrs. Rigney, who once again looked ravishing and delicious, and myself to the gauntlet of surging paparazzi that swarmed the entrance to the casino. Flash bulbs popped incessantly with each famous and infamous arrival.

We eventually made our way in to the casino filled with glamorous movie people from around the globe schmoozing and sipping from the ever-flowing fountain of champagne.

The ballroom also served as an opulent move theatre. No change in seating or table arrangements was necessary. A huge screen was lowered from over the bandstand and everyone sat at his or her respective tables. Each table was festooned with elaborate and beautiful arrangements of tropical flora. Everyone enjoyed the formal setting, and the bill of fare was leaps and bounds above the popcorn and candy found in a standard pleasure palace.

As we mingled, I tried to observe who attended this evening, as was my usual preoccupation at such functions. Sir Arthur was here, again without the company of one Phangs Pa. Sumner Renton, the museum curator was here, as was Mr. Chang and his associate Ahn Hai. I didn't see Blaine Pond or Dr. Con—not that I expected to see either at a film fest. I wouldn't have expected to see Sir Arthur or Mr. Chang in such surroundings, either, yet here they were.

I excused myself from Mrs. Rigney and her adoring acquaintances and strolled to where Sumner Renton stood excitedly amongst the rich and famous. "Good evening, Mr. Renton," I said. "Very exciting evening, isn't it?"

"Oh, yes, Mr. Dugan, it certainly is. It's positively electric. This is one of my favorite festivities on the island. I look forward to this week every year. Rarely do you get this many movie stars and industry people of this caliber on one spot at one time. Cannes may be the only equivalent in the entire world. I'm such a move fan; I can hardly contain my excitement."

I hated to rain on the gay caballero's parade, but there's a party pooper in every crowd, and one must do what one must do. "I understand Harold Peters performed an audit on the inventory in the bird sanctuary this morning?" I asked.

"Well, I'm not certain it was an audit so much, but a case of overt curiosity on Mr. Peter's part, I suspect," he responded. "As I explained to Mr. Peters over the phone when he called to arrange the visit, there is nothing in the sanctuary of the museum that belongs to the Rigney Corporation or the Catalina Cattle Company. As everyone knows, the museum and gallery are separate entities unto themselves."

"So did he find anything of interest?" I asked.

"Actually, he seemed quite interested in seeing everything. He wanted to see every room and storage vault," said the curator with obvious displeasure. "He was very thorough. He looked in every nook and cranny. He may have categorized his visit as an inventory audit; I would call it a random search."

"But you say he didn't seem particularly interested in any specific item," I persisted. "Is it possible that he may have removed something from any of the collections without you knowing it?"

Mr. Renton looked quizzically at me for a brief moment before answering. "No, he didn't seem particularly interested in any one specific item that I could tell. And no, I don't believe he removed anything. Of course, I suppose it's possible that he could have surreptitiously absconded with some small object; after all, he did carry a small satchel with him. But as far as I know, he didn't pilfer anything, if that's what you mean."

I had pushed too far and made Sumner jumpy and suspicious.

"I am curious as to everyone's sudden intense interest in the bird sanctuary and its contents," he said.

"What do you mean?" I asked.

"Well, first Mr. Peters requests a visit under the pretense of some dubious inventory expedition. Then Sir Arthur calls and requests a tour of the sanctuary. And now you express undefined interest as well. I've never had such sudden and feigned interest in the process of the restoration of sunken artifacts in all my days as a curator. Is there something that everybody thinks I should know about?"

"That may well be the case," I responded. "That is what I'm trying to determine. Let me ask you this, Sumner. Did P.K. send back any items from the treasure he was exploring at the time of his disappearance?"

Now the good curator seemed more than puzzled. I wasn't sure if it was just wariness or genuine fright—maybe he was just perturbed. All of the fun seemed to go out of his evening. He began to fidget. He wanted to be somewhere else. Anywhere else. Finally, he said, "What if I was to tell you that he did send back a few items from that expedition? Then what?"

I responded by asking, "Well, did Mr. Peters or Sir Arthur ask you specifically about objects from that collection?"

"No," he answered. "As I told you before, Mr. Peters didn't seem particularly interested in any specific item. As I said before, it appeared to be a random search. If he was looking for anything in particular, I don't think he found it. Do you know what he might have been looking for?"

"I may have an idea, but it is no more than idle speculation at present. You mentioned that P.K. might have indeed sent back objects from his last expedition. Would those items arouse such widespread interest?"

The good curator hesitated once again. His eyes darted around the room. "Mr. Dugan, I'm afraid that was my feeble attempt to learn what everyone seems so interested in. There are many rumors circulating around the island, but I assure you that I have no firsthand knowledge of any such treasure."

"Believe me, Mr. Renton, I don't wish to alarm you. This may be nothing more than misspent curiosity on my part. However, the less you know at this point, the better off you'll be. Therefore, it is nothing I want to concern you with at this time. I would, however, request that I be present on the tour of the sanctuary when Sir Arthur is granted that opportunity."

"I suppose that could be arranged," he said, "but you don't mind if I ask for Mrs. Rigney's concurrence in this matter? After all, she is on the board of directors, and this is a rather unusual request."

"I would hope that you do just that, Mr. Renton," I said. "I think that would be a very prudent idea. In fact, I would hope that Mrs. Rigney might find time in her scheduled to accompany us."

"Very well then, Mr. Dugan," said the good curator. "I shall arrange a visit for you and Sir Arthur that is convenient for Mrs. Rigney, as well. Provided, of course, that she approves the tour in the first place."

"Splendid, Sumner, old chap," I said. "I look forward to it."

With that unpleasantness completed, Sumner Renton scurried off to calmer, more familiar surroundings and a stiff shot of straight bourbon. His pristine, prissy, academic world had been shaken, set askew. The Commodore was right; P.K. would never have entrusted such a clandestine operation to the likes of Sumner Renton. He was too fragile. Under pressure, he would crumble like a stale cookie. He would have sprung sprockets like a cheap watch. He would short circuit quicker than a Japanese transistor radio.

I returned to where Lara Rigney was waiting. The lights began to flicker, signifying the start of the film, so we adjourned to our table and awaited the beginning of the motion picture.

I dozed off occasionally throughout the course of the film, only to be jolted awake by the horrific mastication of one biblical conflagration after another. Lara elbowed me in the ribs several times when my snoring grew louder than the tortured screams emanating from the film as Christians were thrown to the lions, or a competitor was mercilessly pulverized beneath the hooves and wheels of a thundering chariot during an epic race around an immense, gothic hippodrome.

Upon the completion of the film, the audience burst into applause, followed by a standing ovation for the producer, director, and stars. The colossal production was by far more spectacular than anything that had come before. Everything that had come before was "gone with the wind." Wow! Not only had I become a dashing socialite and art connoisseur, I was also capable of astonishingly insightful, substantive analogies of film history. Quite the Renaissance man. Rather full of bologna, wouldn't you say? Who, moi?

It was spectacular film with which to open this year's Avalon International Film Festival. Everyone was obviously impressed and excited. It was indeed a stupendous, star-studded evening on Santa Catalina Island.

As the film screen retracted into the ceiling, the chandeliers slowly illuminated the glittering throngs. The orchestra began to assemble on the stage and preparations were readied for this evening's prime rib roast buffet. Lara and I stepped outside for a breath of fresh air and a smoke. The other attendees had similar inclinations, and the promenade around the casino quickly filled with happy, peppy people.

"So, angel, did you and Mr. Pond have an enjoyable afternoon?" I asked with indignation. She smiled, gave me a sideways glance, and innocently sipped from her champagne flute.

She finally said, "I'll bet you've been just dying to ask me that question, haven't you, Dugan?"

"Yes," I said. "It's been bothering me all afternoon."

"Ha!" she burst out laughing. "You lying dog. Are you trying to bust my chops or what? I know where you were this afternoon, and I know you've been dipping your wick in the family gene pool as well. I doubt you thought about me even once this afternoon, you maniacal cad."

Ouch! Caught with my hand in the cookie jar. What can one say? How does one respond in this position? While I squirmed and fumbled for some meager explanation, of which there, of course, was none, she relieved my anxiety by mercifully answering my original question.

"Yes,' she said. "To answer your pitifully obvious inquiry, Blaine and I enjoyed a wonderful afternoon together. He's very charming and witty," she toyed. "I imagine most women find him extremely handsome and dashingly virile. Don't you think that would be the case, Dugan?"

That's it, you vixen bitch. Just twist that dagger around a few more times, nice and slow, your Royal Viciousness. I said nothing. I stood there silently rocking back and forth, heel to toe, tapping my champagne flute against tightened lips. *Yes, I was pouting again. This babe was a real emotional roller-coaster ride.*

I stared out to sea, occasionally glancing over at her. She made little attempt to conceal her pleasure at my silent suffering. She simply smiled, placed the tip of her finger to her tongue, and began to rub her moistened finger in circular motions around the edge of her glass until a harmonious ring began to emanate from it. Suddenly, almost magically, everyone on the casino promenade began harmonizing with his or her champagne glasses as well. The entire area gently floated on gossamer waves of crystalline chimes. It was enchanting, mystical—almost spiritual. Everyone laughed and applauded at its conclusion. It was a spontaneous—a simultaneous orgasmatron.

We eventually returned to the ballroom and buffet line. Encumbered with succulent eatables, we returned to our table to enjoy the sumptuous feast. Once again, I tried to ease my way into a conversation about her and Blaine Pond. I innocently asked about their tour of the ceramics plant. She told me that

Mr. Pond seemed to enjoy the tour immensely and asked many questions about the operation of the factory. She said he had placed a sizeable order for several tons of Catalina tile, enough to fill several shipping containers bound for the Far East. I finally asked her straight out if Mr. Pond had expressed any curiosity about certain artifacts that might be stored in the bird sanctuary.

"No," she said. "He didn't seem the least bit interested in sunken treasure, artifacts, of anything of that nature. He was genuinely fascinated with the ceramic tile process, and all of his inquires were within that context—that is," she continued, "until we got on the subject of Dr. Con and the guano mine."

"Yes," I responded. "I've noticed Blaine Pond has a certain preoccupation with Dr. Con myself. What type of questions was he asking?"

"Well," she began. "During our drive over the mountain to Smuggler's Cove, I got the impression that Blaine was more familiar with the mysterious Dr. Con than he let on. He wanted to know everything about the operation that I could tell him. When I mentioned Dr. Con's difficulties with the Conservancy Committee and their suspicions regarding his underwater dredging, Blaine was very interested. During the course of our conversation, he revealed that he had inadvertently come across information about a shipment of unusually large sections of flanged steel tubes that were produced in a mill in Eastern Europe and transshipped through Panama, with the final destination being Catalina Island."

"Why would Mr. Pond be interest in a shipment of steel tubing?" I asked.

"He never actually explained why he was interested," she said, "other than the fact that the shipping manifest listed the tubing as oil pumping pipe. He asked if I was aware of a shipment of a large pipe sections arriving on the island.

"I explained that all large cargo, such as that, would have to be shipped to the Port of Los Angeles first and off-loaded onto a barge for delivery across the channel. However, because Dr. Con conducts his own barge operation to the mainland, he could have imported such cargo on his own barges; it would not necessarily arrive at Avalon's shipping dock. He could have delivered it directly to his facilities at Smuggler's Cove."

"That's all interesting enough on its own," I said. "However, I fail to see how that sheds any light on my immediate investigation into the disappearance of your husband."

"I didn't realize it was supposed to shed any light on that subject," she said. "Do you have reason to believe that Dr. Con is connected to Johnny's disappearance?"

"No, nothing in particular," I said. "It's just that there are so many suspicious characters working so many different angles here that it's difficult to untangle the connections."

"I wonder why Blaine Pond is so interested in Dr. Con's endeavors and shipments of oil pipe. There must be something to the rumor of Dr. Con's clandestine underwater sluice-dredger. That invention must have some application other than sucking sand off the bottom of a cove and depositing it somewhere else. There must be other technological applications for such a device to attract the likes of Blaine Pond."

Either way, I failed to see any connection to Johnny's disappearance; however, I felt compelled to look down yet another avenue, just the same.

"Do you think it would be possible for me to use the ski boat tomorrow?" I asked.

"I'm sure that could be arranged," she said. "Plan on doing some skiing?"

"No, more like a little fishing expedition."

Chapter 13

The Fishing Expedition

S paulding awoke me early in the morning, as I had requested. After escorting Mrs. Rigney home from the premiere the previous evening, I stayed on in one of the many guest rooms in the mansion.

I quickly performed the "triple S" morning routine then scanned the assorted outfits in the closet. I had heard somewhere that when you were a guest at Hearst Castle, the Big R provided a complete wardrobe during your stay—from riding boots and pants to bathing suits and towels. He insisted you take it with you when you left. He even provided the valise for the towels and the wardrobe.

The Rigney's were not quite as flamboyant, but they did provide ample outfits for various activities while you were a guest. I rifled through the sporting attire and settled on a pair of khaki trousers and a matching long-sleeved shirt. On the shelf above, I found a crisp, tan ball cap, and on the shoe rack below was a fine pair of nearly new, capable beige boat shoes. An entire outfit.

I cradled the phone receiver under my chin while I rolled up my sleeves and dialed the number to my office. Once again, "Travis Dugan Investigations," sang across the line.

"Good morning, Precious. How are you, my dove?" I chimed.

"Good morning," came her cheery reply. "You sound much more rested and relaxed this morning, Travis."

"Well, I spent all of yesterday lounging aboard a splendid yacht with a cool margarita. Then I topped off the evening attending a Hollywood motion picture premiere and a prime rib roast buffet. This morning, I'm off on a deep-sea fishing trip," I explained.

"Oooh, that sounds great, Travis," she said. "I'm glad you're finally able to relax and enjoy your vacation, for a change."

"So I suppose you want to get to the information you requested and skip the usual banter? Unfortunately," she began, "you could write all the information I was able to gather on the back of a matchbook. Nobody wants to discuss Blaine Pond other than to confirm that he is indeed a purchasing agent for the East-Asian Trading Company. You can garner your own conclusions from that. As I mentioned yesterday, East-Asian is a well known front for British intelligence; therefore, Mr. Pond would most probably function relative to that capacity."

"Likewise," she continued. "Knowing the background of Sir Arthur Sidney and having both gentlemen on the same tiny island in the middle of the Pacific at the same time, is certainly more than just coincidence. Combine that information with the sketchy facts regarding Dr. Con's background, and you can hypothesize some very intriguing theories. From what I gather, which is very little, Dr. Con's expertise is in chemical engineering, with a specialty in explosives and propellants."

"Propellants?" I mistakenly asked aloud. "Like aerosol cans?"

"No, asshole. What's an aerosol can? Propellants! Propellants! From the word, 'propel'? As in propulsion? Rocket fuel, missile propulsion—shit like that. You put Blaine Pond, Sir Arthur, and Dr. Con in the same place, at the same time, and it makes you wonder, doesn't it?"

"Yes, that does cause one to ponder. What about Mr. Chang?" I asked.

"Nothing on Mr. Chang at this time. If he does represent the Chinese government, no one in regular diplomatic circles knows of him. I'm sorry I couldn't be more helpful, but these guys are pretty far out on the fringes of my usual information loop."

"That's fine, doll face," I said. "Every little bit helps. While you're at it, here are a couple more names for you. The first is Harold Peters. Male, Caucasian, brown and brown, five-six, one hundred seventy-five points. Approximately forty to forty-five. He's an accountant with some outfit in Chicago, conducting an audit for the Rigney Corporation. Strange little guy. Speaks in an anxiety-ridden hush.

"The second guy's name is Sumner Renton. Male, Caucasian, brown and brown, five-seven, one hundred sixty-five pounds, thirty to thirty-five. He's presently the curator of the Avalon Museum and Art Gallery. Both of these fish are soft targets," I explained. "Pansy-ass sissy boys. I doubt either one of them could break a sweat in a Scandinavian sauna bath. But you know how these quiet unassuming types are—Harvey Milktoast one day, then they snap and they're Jack the Ripper the next."

"Yes, that's one vacation ya got goin' for yourself, Travis. Black market arms smugglers, British spies, Tong gangsters, casino playboys, and Hiram Holliday frustrated momma's boys. Not to mention the odd assassin or two or the assorted waterfront misfits. Not your typical vacation brochure types, huh, Studley Do-right?"

"You got that right, sweetheart. This is the oddest collection of misguided, misbegotten miscreants I've seen in some time. Wish me luck on my fishing trip."

I met Consuela downstairs in the kitchen, where I grabbed a cup of coffee and butter and honey-laden tortilla. She informed me that Manuel, her husband, and Senorita Rigney had already gone down to the boat to put in the fuel and buy the bait for the day's outing.

I strolled down the tree-lined drive through the estate and down the hill to the boat dock. Consuela had informed me before I left the mansion that, much to my relief, Lara Rigney would be busy the entire day with meetings, and luncheons with the various dignitaries associated with the foreign part of the film festival and would not be, therefore, cavorting with the nauseatingly dashing Blaine Pond.

Upon my arrival at the dock, both Rita and the boat were ready for action—the fast and wet variety. Manuel cast off the lines, and Rita powered the boat expertly away from the dock and out to the open ocean. Avalon disappeared in our wake as we headed south past the rock quarry and on around the southern tip of the island toward Seal Cove.

Rita wore a short cropped man's undershirt, paper thin, and the shortest shorts I'd ever seen. Her dark, smooth skin glistened in the morning sun as she maneuvered the boat like a seasoned boatswain's mate.

As we approached Seal Cove, Rita slowed the boat, quietly shut off the motor, and removed her t-shirt and shorts, revealing the world's smallest bathing suit. It was little more than three band-aids strung together with dental floss. She was gorgeous. The material, what little there was, was thin white silk.

As we bobbed in the swell just off Seal Cove, Rita reached in the bait bucket and withdrew several handfuls of live shad, which she tossed overboard to the curious sea lions. They darted under and around the boat like sleek brown torpedoes. Dozens of dark-eyed sea lions lifted their smooth heads above the surface as Rita prepared to join them in the water with a small net bag of live shad.

She stepped onto the transom and in one smooth motion dove effortlessly beneath the waves. The dominant bulls barked their displeasure from the beach for the intrusion into their courtship rituals taking place along the sandy shores.

Rita swam like a graceful mermaid. She hand-fed each sea lion as it gently approached then darted away with her offering. It was obvious that this was a bond forged over a lifetime with graciousness, affection, and respect. Upon her emergence from the water, Rita's bathing suit had the transparent qualities of wet toilet paper, exposing every dimple and fold of her magnificently firm and glistening body. So natural. So innocent. So arousing.

Rita toweled herself, settled into the seat, powered up the boat, and we were off. In a great roar of engine and swirl of bubbling, white water, we headed toward the south end of the island to the windward side—destination, Smuggler's Cove.

As we approached the entrance to the cove, we noticed a small fishing boat anchored approximately one hundred yards to the south of the heavily posted entrance. We continued past the small boat and anchored several hundred yards beyond, near the north side of the cove entrance. Once we were secure at anchor, I baited a hook and cast the line. I set my reel and settled in for a quiet afternoon of quasi-fishing.

I removed my shirt and deck shoes then stripped down to my BVDs. I removed the binoculars Consuela had provided and began to leisurely survey the area. The other boat had one Mexican deck hand aboard, and the flag he flew indicated a diver in the water. The cove appeared relatively quiet, as was to be expected during daylight hours. The Chinese guards at the entrance, however, seemed keenly aware of our activities. They were scanning both boats through powerful binoculars.

I casually returned the binoculars to their case and decided to lay low for a while and be a little less obvious, acting more like an insignificant fisherman lolling away the daylight with his lovely, dark girlfriend.

I gazed over to where Rita lay reclined on a spongy mat stretched along the deck in the bottom of the boat. She had re-moved the top of her bathing suite and was peacefully absorbing the sun's warm rays, erect nipples majestically reach-ing toward the soft blue sky. I though better of it, but was unable to restrain myself. I confidently lowered myself from the seat to the dark, lustrous body and proceeded to unleash the pangs of desire. In the heat of passion, it may have seemed more like rape, but she didn't seem to mind. She didn't seem to mind several times. Eventually, a role reversal occurred, and she assumed the role of aggressor. I didn't seem to mind—didn't seem to mind several times.

Upon the conclusion of our interlude, and I do mean 'lewd,' I slowly sat up and peered over the side toward the other boat. The diver had emerged from the water and was scanning the ocean in our direction. I retrieved the binoculars and raised them to my eyes. I stared directly into the pair of binoculars that the diver in the other boat had fixed upon our position. I waved playfully to the ardent voyeur. He lowered his binoculars and I recognized him clearly. To my surprise, it was Blaine Pond. By the look on his face, I guessed that he was not particularly thrilled to see me. He mouthed a rather disgusting expletive in my direction and then feverishly began to make ready to depart. The deck hand quickly raised anchor, and Pond had the craft underway and heading in our direction at full speed. I slipped my shorts back on, nonchalantly lit Rita and myself a cigarette, and awaited Pond's imminent arrival]

He didn't stop, however; instead, he blew by us at high speed, tossing our boat about violently with his wake. He went by us so close that he almost fouled our anchor line, and as he passed, he made a very rude hand gesture, for which I gesticulated in kind, adding verbal emphasis with regard to his British propensity toward same gender sex.

Rita laughed at my sophomoric outburst. "Don't you know he's a British secret agent?" she said. "He'll probably kick your ass when we get back."

"Oh, yeah?" I retorted. "I welcome the opportunity to whip his queer-bait Limey butt. What's his problem, anyway? It's a big ocean, and I can fish anywhere I damn well please."

"Fish, smish," she replied, apparently unimpressed with my contrived bravado. "Pish, posh, yadda-yadda, calm down. We all know why we're all out here. And it sure ain't for the fishin'," she said. "You're just pissed off 'cause he boinked your girlfriend yesterday."

"How do you know he boinked Lara yesterday?" I responded. "And how do you know that he's a British agent?"

She just looked at me knowingly and smiled. "It's a small island, Travis," she said. "Surely you've heard that before?"

We spent the remainder of the afternoon relaxing in the warm sun, and actually managed to catch a few keepers, pausing occasionally to observe the activities in Smuggler's Cove. For the most part, the goings-on within Dr. Con's compound seemed pretty ordinary and commonplace for a mining operation. There was no apparent clandestine activity, no stockpiles of steel tubing, and no evidence of dredging or anything that could be considered unusual. There was continual barge traffic in and out of the cove as they conveyed the guano from stockpiles on shore, but the actual mining operations were suspended during daylight hours, when the bats were in residence.

As the sun began to fade, we weighed anchor and headed back to Avalon. I casually attempted to extract information from Rita about Nicky Fallon during our ride home. My impression was that Rita and Nicky shared a relationship of convenience. She was not particularly infatuated with him, nor was she in love.

Rita was a realist. She knew that many of her relationships were based on her personal wealth, her family's stature in the world, and their preeminence here on the island. Many of her suitors were gold-digging gigolos, concerned only with fortunes gained through a relationship with the Commodore's daughter. They had no concern for her feelings or happiness. She was well aware of their superficiality and had come to terms with it. She believed that Nicky Fallon sought comfort and security in their relationship, not so much the building of his own fortune. He desired respectability. He strived for acceptance by the island community and members of her immediate family—specifically, her brother Johnny and her father, the Commodore.

For her part, she felt that Nicky Fallon treated her well and didn't try to take advantage of her. He wasn't overly possessive, as many of her former beaus were wont to be, and he allowed her the freedom and space to conduct and enjoy life as she wished.

She was wild and rebellious as a teenager, and the island had seemed confining, more like prison than paradise. Now she had, for the most part, resigned herself to the reality that her life probably would not change appreciably whether she remained single for the rest of her life or Prince Charming came riding in on his gallant white steed and swept her off her feet. She would remain on the island, and her daily activities would change very little. Her acquiescence did not come with the baggage of regret. She would have it no other way. She would carry out the duties and responsibilities afforded her station. She was not the Princess of Monaco, but the prominence of her family required a certain obligation and reliability on her part. This was as she wished. She had grown up, attained discernable maturity, and was content with her life. She was fortunate and knew it. She felt no compulsion to venture much beyond the foreseeable horizon. I envied her contentment.

Chapter 14

The Big One That Got Away and Other Fishy Stories

L ara Rigney and I arrived at the casino just after dark amid the jostling glitz we had experienced the previous evenings.

The film this evening was a French production, and the introductions involved much hugging and kissing. I tended to withdraw from such behavior when the participants were of the male species and made a concerted effort to avoid all introductions.

Once I ensconced Lara at her table, I graciously excused myself and quietly retired to the gaming room; though the crowd upstairs was only slightly smaller than previous evenings, they were no less animated.

I spotted Nicky Fallon at the far end of the bar, engaged in a heated conversation with a short, nattily attired older man. The older man was furiously jabbing a finger at the seemingly bewildered Nicky Fallon. The expression on the older man's face was stern and direct. Nicky responded as if attempting to offer some kind of excuse; it involved a lot of shoulder shrugging and hand wringing. It appeared as though he was being called on the carpet for some shortcoming or indiscretion. I couldn't imagine a cum laude Adonis like Nicky Fallon capable of shortcomings or indiscretions, but that's how it looked.

I casually strolled in their direction, attempting to eavesdrop on the conversation. When I got within earshot, I realized the entire exercise was to no avail. They were speaking Sicilian, and I had not a clue as to what was being so aggressively discussed.

I hovered a bit too long, I suppose, as they decided to continue their conversation in a more secluded location. I followed at a discreet distance as they exited the gaming room and adjourned to the mezzanine office downstairs.

I watched furtively through the window as the discussion between the two men grew more and more angry. Their voices grew increasingly louder, accompanied by vigorous arm waving and rude hand gestures rife with backhand flicking under the chin and similar thumb snaps from the top front teeth. I'm sure there's an appropriate ethnic phrase to describe this exercise, but hey, I'm from L.A.

The boisterous exchange culminated with Nicky Fallon escorting the shorter man to the door by means of the back of his collar and the seat of his britches. I barely had time to retreat to a darkened corner of the alcove before the door flew open and the Pizan was unceremoniously tossed out on the sidewalk. The door then slammed shut with much prejudice.

The man slowly got to his feet, brushed himself off, and straightened his tie. He turned toward the door and brought his index finger across his throat from ear to ear and muttered one of the few Italian words I do happen to understand—"morta"—death. I remained concealed in the darkness as the man returned upstairs to the gaming room.

I returned to my original position from which I had spied upon the argument. I couldn't see Nicky Fallon anywhere inside. I tried the door; it was locked. I reached in the pocket of my jacket and withdrew my standard-issue burglar tools—two small metal rods, bent at ninety degrees about three-quarters down their length. They looked like small, thin Allen wrenches. I slipped the rods in the lock and within seconds, the door opened, and I quietly stepped inside.

The interior office was very dark, except for a thin shard of light appearing from under Nicky Fallon's office door. I crept to the door and placed my ear against it. From what I could hear, he was shuffling through desk drawers. Then he sat down and began to dial the phone. I counted the return clicks as he spun the dial. It was an L.A. number. I jotted it down, and continued to listen intently.

Once again, the conversation was in Sicilian; I was able to decipher only a few words—something about time, or more time, and big hands, or fists, or maybe heavy hands—something like that.

At the end of a rather excited conversation, Nicky slammed the phone down and trashed his office in a heated rage. Discretion being the better part of valor, I seized the opportunity to make my exit. I stepped back outside to the shadows just as the short man and his no-necked, refrigerator-sized friend emerged from the casino and hailed a cab. If it walked like a duck and it quacked like a duck, it must be a duck. These two walked and quacked like wise guys. I had an impulse to duck.

I hurried down the ramp to grab a cab of my own and follow them. Before I reached the bottom, a hulking figure jumped out of the darkness and cold-cocked me, knocking me to the ground.

"You clumsy bastard," he said. "What the bloody hell do you think you're doing shlepping around in the middle of my business?" It was a very angry Blaine Pond.

I jumped to my feet just in time to catch a sidekick square in the chest, knocking me breathless to the pavement again. This time, I jumped to my feet and ducked under a furious spinning back kick. I then planted a well-placed kick of my own deep in his groin, sending him to the ground in agony. He rolled to the bottom of the ramp in a tight fetal ball, clutching his crotch, and then miraculously sprang off the ground like a gazelle into an upright fighting stance. Remarkable recuperative powers. I suspected him to be a gelding.

He rushed toward me with a barrage of punches and kicks, attempting to steamroll me. I countered with a head-butting charge of my own, and we came together in a jumble, finally crashing to the ground, elbows over assholes.

I throttled him with my left hand, pummeling his rib cage with a jackhammer of a right. We continued to wrestle down the promenade, altering from clean, short shots to schoolyard scuffling, until we eventually crashed through the newsstand souvenir vendors at the highly illuminated casino entrance, amid throngs of foreign paparazzi and horrified filmgoers.

I kept him close to try to nullify his spinning back kicks and elaborate karate techniques. Seemed like everybody, from spindly old ladies to snot-nosed street punks knew this Oriental martial arts crap. I'd gotten my butt kicked on numerous occasions by the most unlikely of malcontents. I hate when that happens.

We continued to scuffle amongst the well-lit, beautiful people until Constable LaFarge arrived on the scene with his band of merry mercenaries, who proceeded to whack the hell out of us with their wickedly persuasive batons. I don't mean the kind of batons that heavy-thighed young cheerleaders tossed spinning into the air during parades or football halftimes. I mean heavy, black truncheons that pulverize bones and pulp flesh.

The cadre of sadistic Gendarmes rudely, but efficiently, hustled us off to a waiting paddy wagon and trundled us away to the Victorian hoosegow, where we cooled our heels and our tempers for what seemed an eternity.

While Pond and I nursed our respective bruises, we came to terms and agreed that a cooperation pact might be more prudent and less abusive to our own well-being. Since we were not apparently after the same prey, perhaps we could pool our resources and cover more territory in less time, to the benefit of both.

Sometime, I guessed around midnight, the phone rang and Constable LaFarge, who had just returned, answered. He turned toward my cell and said to whoever was on the other end, "Dugan? Yes, I believe I could find him for you. Hold the line a moment." LaFarge turned to me and asked, "Do you know an Inspector Lugar, L.A. P.D.?"

Lugar and I went back a long way. He was a fair guy, a fine cop, and he always gave me a square shake—a commodity not always in stock when the boys with badges associated with us free-lancers. We weren't necessarily bosom buddies, but we had shared a couple of drinks and a couple of sorrows in the past, and we treated each other with a degree of respect. He was, for the most part, a conscientious detective and a straight shooter. I liked the guy and thought him honorable and true to his word.

I nodded in the affirmative to LaFarge, and he brought the phone over and passed it through the cell bars.

"This is Dugan," I said.

"Well, it didn't take very long to find you," Lugar said. "I presume that, as usual, you're already in custody?"

"Yes, I seem to be taking up residence here," I responded. "I'm thinking of redecorating. I have swatches."

"I have some bad news for you," he said. "Your secretary was assaulted in your office a couple of hours ago. The cleaning lady found her. She'll be all right; we've taken her to the hospital. She doesn't appear seriously hurt—no permanent damage. She looks like she's been slapped around pretty good, though. Whoever it was, they turned your office upside down. Got any ideas as to who or why?" he asked.

"She was checking backgrounds on several suspects in a missing person's investigation," I responded. "But I'm not at liberty to divulge those names at present, if you know what I mean. I'll be glad to give you the run-down when I'm able to call from a more secure location."

"I understand," he said. "Would the name Gerald Bull be on your list of suspects?" he asked.

"Gerald Bull?" I repeated. "No, I'm not aware of that name at all. Why?"

"I penciled over some impressions left in the notepad by the phone," he explained. "The top sheet that you secretary had written on was gone, but she left impressions on the second page. Gerald Bull was the name that appeared. And something called HARP."

I thanked Lugar for calling me. I assured him I would call him in the morning, by which time I assumed I would be back out on the street. I hung up the phone and passed it back through the bars.

Blaine Pond motioned me over to where our two cells joined. "Forgive me for eavesdropping," he said. "But did I hear you mention the name Gerald Bull?"

I paused. Gerald Bull. Gerald Bull. Who the hell is Gerald Bull? I had never heard of the guy, yet both Blaine Pond and my secretary seemed to have some interest in him.

I answered in my usual manner—with a question of my own. "Do you have some information on that name?

"I believe we should have a drink somewhere when we are released," he said. "We may have some commonality on the island after all."

LaFarge returned and opened our cell doors. We were taken to his office where he returned our personal possessions, including our weapons. Pond's being a 9 mm Beretta. Very chic.

"I'm giving you gentlemen fair warning," began La-Farge. "We have taken the liberty of test-firing each of your weapons. Should matching slugs be found lodged in some unfortunate recipient here on the island, believe me, you will be hammered for it. Do I make myself perfectly clear, gentlemen?"

We both agreed and apologized for our juvenile behavior earlier in the evening, apologizing in the most humble and repentant manner we could muster. The inspector just shook his head in disgust. I'm sure he was thinking that this was not the last he had seen of us.

He motioned to his lieutenant, who opened the door to the outer office and hustled us back out onto the sidewalk. We apparently were free to go. Just as unceremoniously as we had arrived.

Pond and I walked down to the oceanfront boardwalk then over to the casino. It was a cool evening, and a light mist was beginning to roll in off the dark sea.

We found Roscoe and his cab in the usual place. We casually leaned on the cab, our tattered remains of once-fine fabric soiled and shredded. We waited, the three of us, for Lara Rigney to emerge at the conclusion of the film and dining fest. When she finally did, she paused, and as she walked over to where we waited, shook her head in amused disgust, much as Inspector LaFarge had done only minutes earlier.

"Well, if you two aren't a couple of pathetic looking zots," she said. "What have you saps been up to?"

"We were merely discussing which of us would have the honor of accompanying you for a nightcap," responded the resilient Blaine Pond.

"Yes," I infused. "And came to a somewhat reluctant compromise."

"Gosh boys, I suppose I should be flattered. Under more appealing circumstances I probably would be, even though I think both of you are full of shit. Be that as it may, it's late, I'm tired, and you two are grinnin' like a couple of old maids playing squat-tag in an asparagus patch. So if you'd be so kind as to escort me home, I'd be ever so grateful—y'all."

W'all climbed into the cab and made the short journey to the estate. Once we had delivered Lara safely, we had Roscoe drop us off at the Blue Parrot, which was again the usual bastion of upscale scalawags. We grabbed a booth at the far end of the bar. Chin Lee arrived to take our order, but before I had a chance to acknowledge her, she placed her finger in front of her pursed lips, indicating not to act as though we were acquainted. Pond ordered a martini—shaken, not stirred. I put up two fingers. She bowed and departed. Very odd.

Pond waited until Chin Lee delivered our drinks before beginning. Chin Lee did not look at me and quickly departed. Pond wasted no time.

"I am investigating a consortium of underground weapons designers and propulsion engineers that may be involved in a clandestine operation to construct a massive cannon capable of sending a large projectile several hundred miles. Gerald Bull is pivotal in that investigation. He is a rogue weapons designer specializing in large caliber artillery. We have reason to believe that he is in possession of specifications and has components manufactured in various locations throughout the world, with which to build an immense artillery piece called 'the Super Gun.'"

"You see, Mr. Dugan, the problem with large, conventional, single-detonation cannon has always been size of detonation relative to weight and range of projectile. The finest deck guns on the biggest battleship afloat today can, at best, deliver a payload roughly the size of a small automobile twenty to twenty-five miles. No one has yet developed a breach capable of containing more explosive power without destroying the artillery piece itself. It simply blows itself apart. However," he continued. "If one developed a propulsion system that produced a series of smaller, simultaneous detonations as the projectile progressed through the barrel of the weapon, the distance or range of such a system would theoretically be ten-fold what a present-day, single-detonation weapon could achieve. Likewise, the longer the barrel the projectile traverses, the more detonations can occur, thereby increasing velocity at the point of exit. Theoretically, the range is endless. Do you realize the ramifications of this new technology, Mr. Dugan?"

"A bigger gun with a heavier payload from farther away," I said. "Isn't that the ultimate goal in all weapons development programs?"

"A bigger gun, heavier payload, from farther away," Pond repeated condescendingly. "That's the most simplistic understatement of the century, you silly bastard. We're talking about completely new and formidable technology, damn it. Don't you see? With weapons such as this, any third-world camel-jockey despot could annihilate his hapless neighbor and disrupt the world's balance of power. You place a nerve gas or any number of biological warheads on the end of that projectile, and you've created a poor man's nuclear missile."

"So, as I understand it, you believe Gerald Bull has specs on a gigantic super gun, and you also have reason to believe that manufactured components of this gun are in transit, the final destination Catalina Island?" I asked.

"Yes, that is the information that I have at this time. Unfortunately, we lost track of the gun components, and Gerald Bull, as well."

"Did you find any evidence here on the island to support your suspicions?" I asked.

"That, my friend, is what I was attempting to determine today before I was so rudely interrupted. However, I found no evidence of underwater activity. Nor did I find any evidence of materials used in the manufacture or construction of artillery weapons. It's a riddle, hidden in a mystery, wrapped in an enigma."

About then, we both noticed the rotund one, Sir Arthur, enter the establishment. He acknowledged our presence with a polite tip of his bowler, but continued past to a table in the corner.

Pond prepared to leave, but before he went, he cautioned me about Sir Arthur. He explained that Sir Arthur was likely to be following the same trail he himself was, but Sir Arthur was not bound by ethics, codes of honor, loyalty to the crown, or any other civilized restriction. "He is ruthless, vicious, depraved, and has no loyalty to king or country. He comes from a highly respected aristocratic family, but then, so did Jack the Ripper. Sir Arthur's influence could have worldwide consequences. He is evil incarnate, Mr. Dugan. Keep your eyes open, lest he pluck them out." With that bit of sage advice, Blaine Pond took his leave, destination unknown.

I finished my drink and picked up the napkin on which it had been setting. Wrapped inside the napkin was a photograph. The picture was apparently taken inside the dining room of the casino. There were several people sitting around a table, only two of which I immediately recognized—Nicky Fallon and Johnny Rigney. Written on the inside of the napkin was a note that said, "Do not attempt to contact me. I will find you."

Chin Lee undoubtedly placed the photo and the note there, but the reason was puzzling. As was her demeanor. She was cautious, wary, and scared. I looked around the room for her, but she was nowhere to be seen. Sir Arthur got up from where he had been seated and came toward me. I stuffed the photo and note into my pocket as he approached.

"Good evening, Mr. Dugan," he said. "Or perhaps it would be more accurate to say 'good morning.' May I join you, sir?"

I nodded and motioned for him to take the seat across from me. He was beginning to annoy me. Everywhere I went, he seemed to show up. He was a big windbag, but he revealed some interesting facts.

"So, Mr. Dugan, I see that you've made the acquaintance of my worthy and cunning baccarat opponent—the benevolent Blaine Pond."

"Yes, we met previously at the museum. He had some very nice things to say about you, Sir Arthur."

"Yes, indeed, Mr. Dugan. I'm sure he did. From the looks of your rather disheveled attire, my friend, I conclude that your most recent introduction was not an entirely civil reunion?"

"Oh, it's not quite as tragic as first appearances would have you believe," I explained. "We merely had a small misunderstanding regarding the affections of a certain lady, who shall remain anonymous. But we settled our differences amiably and have agreed to conduct ourselves as gentlemen from here on—much easier on the wardrobe."

He lowered his voice to insure confidentiality. "So, my friend, have you considered my proposal from yesterday regarding the quest for the Kubla Khan treasure?"

"Well, Sir Arthur," I began. "I'm not sure I have completely resolved my dilemma regarding conflict of interest, client confidentiality, etcetera. However, I see no harm in sharing information, provided it does not impugn my client's reputation or character, or embarrass the family. I have one other burr in my saddle," I continued. "There are apparently several other individuals immersed in this mystery and parallel conspiracies have emerged; I'm afraid I have serious reservations regarding your methods and integrity."

"Ahhh, my friend," he chortled. "You sound like my chastened compatriot Mr. Pond. Mr. Pond may not agree with my methods, or admire my character, but he can't dispute my results. After all, Mr. Dugan, how do you suppose Mr. Pond found his way to this tiny island? His superiors initiated his activities and inquiries in this location because of information supplied by me! Mr. Pond may be envious of my independence, but I can assure you, he is reluctantly dependant upon my expertise and the integrity of my information. Although Mr. Pond is reluctant to admit it, he labors under a symbiotic, love-hate relationship. Well then, my friend. I hope that alleviates some of your anxiety. I look forward to a successful and profitable conclusion to our search. Oh, by the by," he continued, "I have been contacted by Mr. Sumner, the museum curator. He informs me that a tour of the artifacts in the bird pavilion has been arranged for this afternoon. I understand that you and Mrs. Rigney will be attending as well. I anticipate an extraordinary afternoon. So until then, my friend, I bid you adieu."

With that, Sir Arthur tipped his bowler and trundled from the Blue Parrot. Once again, destination unknown.

Chapter 15

The Bird Pavilion

I was awakened the next morning by the incessant ringing of the phone at the end of the hall. It mercifully interrupted the continuous wartime nightmares that invaded every night's sleep. Tonight's installment was the dead stick, high-speed dive in an attempt to extinguish the engine fire before it severed the right wing. I awoke in the familiar cold sweat, arms and neck muscle-fatigued from tension, short of breath, and paralyzed with terror. I often wondered how I ever survived those missions—or why?

I recognized Mrs. O'Malley's unorthodox gait as she ascended the stairs and eventually made her way to the phone. She spoke briefly, then came down the hall and knocked lightly on my door. "It's young Miss Rigney," she said through the door.

I thanked her, pulled on a pair of trousers, and made my way down the hall to the phone. It was Rita, calling from the boathouse. She wanted me to come down right away. She had something to show me. Rita's tone was not "come hither"; she wanted to show me something, but she was concerned about something.

I showered and dressed as quickly as I could, then made my way across town to where the Rigneys' boats were kept. When I arrived, she took me over to *The Lucky Dutchman*, the Commodore's yacht, and pointed out the telltale scratches around the keyhole on the door.

"This is the way I found it this morning," she said. "The door was open and everything aboard has been searched."

We continued together through each compartment on the boat. "Is anything missing?" I asked.

"Nothing appears missing," she said. "But everything has been handled or inspected, then replaced."

"Is there anything of great value aboard that might interest someone?"

"No," she answered. "There hasn't been anything aboard of value, like paintings or artwork, for years. The boat has not been used in some time."

It appeared to be another seemingly random search, much like the one at the mansion a few nights ago. Furthermore, though they appeared random, the searches were, in fact, in pursuit of specific items. Identity unknown.

"Do you have any idea, or guess, as to what they could be searching for?" I asked.

She put a finger to her lip and looked around, shaking her head slowly. "No, nothing that I can think of."

I removed the photo that I had received last night and showed it to Rita. "Do you recognize anyone in this picture besides Nicky Fallon and Johnny?"

Rita gazed intently at the photo for a few moments. "Well," she began. "The other two men seated at the table—one is a Hollywood movie producer and the other a high-powered agent. The two women are their wives. They are a couple of high rollers, fondly catered to when at the casino. Their hotel accommodations are frequently comped when they stay for any period of time." She paused and looked at the photo more intently. "The man in the background, partially obscured by the hooker with the big hair, I believe is Nicky's Uncle Dominick," she continued. "At least, that is how he was introduced to me."

I took the picture and stared at the man that Rita was referring to. I hadn't looked at the picture last night beyond the people in the foreground. A cold chill ran down my spine. That was Uncle Dominick all right. Only I knew him as Dominick "Nick the Pick" Licatta—Los Angeles mob under-boss who had worked his way up and paid his dues through the ranks of the Johnny Rosselli crime family as an enforcer and hit man. He acquired his sobriquet from the particularly gruesome method by which he dispatched his intended victims—an ice pick through the side of the head. The ice pick never killed the victim straightaway. Instead, they performed a grotesque hemorrhagic ballet of convulsive spasms. It induced a lingering, agonizing death. It was a particularly grisly scene to come upon, something you don't soon forget. And that, of course, is the intention.

This was a stunning and disconcerting revelation. It put a whole new spin on the affair. Nick Licatta was a very scary and extremely vicious individual. He was not somebody to fool around with. Nick the Pick was a very bad guy.

"Does Uncle Dominick visit the island very often?" I asked, trying desperately to mask my anxious voice and quivering kneecaps.

"No, I've only seen him one time, and that was several years ago, when Nicky first came to work for Johnny," she responded.

I thanked Rita for calling me and asked her to inform Constable LaFarge of the break-in. I told her I would see her later and made a hasty departure. I was in a hurry to get back to town and find a phone.

The telephone booth was at the end of the boardwalk, south of town. I gave the operator the number to Inspector Lugar's and while I waited to be connected, searched my pockets for the phone number I had surreptitiously noted last night in Nicky Fallon's outer office.

When Lugar finally came on the line, I gave him the run down on my investigation and the list of names my secretary was working on. After a brief dissertation on what a mess I'd gotten myself into, he informed me that he had checked on Precious Goodlay this morning. She was conscious and recuperating nicely. I thanked him once again for his compassion and concern then asked if he could discreetly look into the recent whereabouts of one Dominick "Nick the Pick" Licatta and the origin of the phone number I had acquired last night.

After a long thoughtful pause, he agreed to do me that favor without inquiring why. He simply cautioned me about stepping on my extremity and hung up the phone. That was the second time I had been warned about that phenomenon, and I was beginning to experience subliminal stomach and groin pains. Maybe it was just hunger. I went in search of a café.

I found an empty stool at the counter, next to Captain Wally, in Skully's waffle joint. Skully's was the morning spot for local fishermen and harbor roustabouts.

"Well, polliwog," said the old crust. "I see you've managed to survive your visit to the island so far. Hugh Polliwog?"

"There're enough intriguing characters here to film a Bogart movie," I responded.

"Speaking of intriguing characters," joked the old salt. "Let me introduce you to my friend Steve Canyon. Steve owns the sea plane service that operates from Wilmington to Avalon."

I reached across the captain and shook hands. Steve Canyon was straight out of the *Terry and the Pirates* comic strip. He was big and blonde, and his salt-water tanned physique fit smartly into his familiar fly-boy khakis.

The waitress brought over a cup of coffee and took my order. I pulled out the photo and handed it to Captain Wally. "Do you recognize anyone in this picture?" I asked. "Besides Nicky Fallon and Johnny Rigney?"

The old man held it out at arm's length, brought it closer, and then farther away again, squinting to focus. "Nope. Sorry," he replied. "All I can tell you is that the photograph was probably taken by Chin Lee when she was the photo-girl at the casino."

"What can you tell me about Chin Lee?" I asked.

"Well, now, that's a very sad tale," he began. "Chin Lee was orphaned at a young age and has been ostracized by the Chinese on the island because of her mixed race. She and Johnny were inseparable as children, and it grew to puppy love when they got a little older. Chin Lee adored Johnny, and he felt the same for her. As time passed, they became lovers and wanted to get married. Unfortunately, it was a Romeo and Juliet situation and doomed from the start. Because of who Johnny was, his family would not allow a union between the young heir-apparent and some mixed-race immigrant orphan. It's a very sad story, and we all feel sorry for Chin Lee."

I sat quietly sipping my coffee and contemplating that bit of information. Now I knew why Chin Lee expressed such anguish the night I walked her home from the Blue Parrot. What did she want from me? Comfort, hope, justice—revenge?

I inhaled the rest of my breakfast, bid good day to the captain and Steve Canyon, then walked the short distance to the casino's office mezzanine.

Upon entering Harold Peter's empty cubicle, I asked the bevy of comely secretaries his whereabouts. They informed me that they had not seen or heard from him since his tour of the artifacts at the bird pavilion. The hair began to stand on the back of my neck again.

The secretaries further informed me that there had been several calls from Harold Peter's office in Chicago. He apparently was supposed to have checked in upon his arrival to the island, but failed to do so. I returned to Peter's office and dialed the number to the Glenmore Hotel. I asked the desk clerk if Mr. Peters was in, or if they had seen him leave this morning. I received a negative response to both inquiries. Next, I phoned the operator and asked that she connect me with Saint Mary's Hospital in L.A. After several extension changes, I was connected with Precious Goodlay's room.

We chatted briefly about her condition; the prognosis was good, and her release from the hospital was imminent. I asked about the assault, and she told me that she hadn't recognized either of her two assailants, but they were your typical knuckle-dragging Neanderthals. They turned the office inside out, took a few notes and files, and left. She said that when she was released from the hospital, she would return to the office and see if she could determine what they had taken.

I apologized for my shortsightedness; I should have recognized the possible threat of assault upon our files and whoever was present. I told her I would see her as soon as I could, and not to worry about the office, it wasn't going anywhere.

I hung up the phone then proceeded to search Harold Peter's office. I found nothing unusual except that he kept his desk locked. That wasn't a problem a bent paper clip couldn't solve. Still, nothing of importance or anything to provide a lead to where my amphibious-looking friend might be found.

I left the casino and walked up Whitley Avenue to Chin Lee's flat. I knocked on the door. No response. I went around and looked in all the windows. No one was home, and the place seemed to be in order. No disarray, but no signs of Chin Lee, either.

I spent the next hour or so at the yacht club. The sailboat regatta was to begin tomorrow and the harbor in front of the yacht club was already brimming with state-of-the-art racing yachts of every size and description. The yacht club itself was abuzz with boat owners, crews, and assorted sporting celebrities, here to partake in regatta festivities. Tonight was the closing night of the film festival, and tomorrow the island's celebration would shift to the yacht club.

I sat nursing a bloody mary, pondering the status of my investigation. Some investigation. I felt like a half-wit stumblebum. There were so many suspicious characters on the island, and such a jumble of conspiracies, that it was becoming impossible to tell the players or their teams without a program. I was beginning to doubt that I could ever unravel the convergent plot twists. I needed to stay focused on my original task. Find out what they were tying so desperately to conceal.

Dr. Con and Blain Pond's investigation centered on the activities associated with the mining operation on the other side of the island. At this point, Pond's investigation had not come up with anything conclusive on his big gun theory. I couldn't see how that saga could have involved Johnny Rigney, at least not at this stage. As far as the Conservancy Committee's suspicions of Dr. Con's alleged dredging of Smuggler's Cove, that, too, would not have involved Johnny to the extent that someone would kill him. No, I thought Johnny Rigney's disappearance had more to do with the casino operations, or the existence of the Kubla Khan treasure. Perhaps I could learn something tangible this afternoon during the tour of the bird pavilion.

I was very concerned about Chin Lee, however. She was apprehensive last night, and she obviously knew more about Johnny's disappearance than one would have guessed, but what? Why did she secrete the photo to me and include the note about not contacting her? Was she deliberately trying to steer me in a certain direction? If so, why didn't she just tell me? Maybe she didn't really know what was relevant and what wasn't. Blaine Pond was right. It was a riddle, hidden in a mystery, wrapped in an enigma. Whatever that is.

And then there's Harold Peters. Has something happened to him, as well? What about Mr. Chang and his smarmy cohort? I hadn't seen them around in several days now. People were beginning to quietly disappear. Add Dominick Licatta to the mix, and we begin to enter a very dark, sinister place. I had better be careful not to step on my prehensile appendage.

I paid the cabin boy his tab and made my way outside. I found Roscoe in his usual location, and together we made the familiar run up through the estate to the mansion, where we would retrieve Lara Rigney then return to town and head toward the airport for our tour of the pavilion.

Lara wore a sort of safari jumpsuit with canvas boat shoes. Her hair was swept back and tied under a broad headband. She was prepared to wade through swamps or tide pools, perhaps machete her way through a steaming jungle.

It was a pleasant ride up the hill to the bird park overlooking Avalon Harbor and the deep, blue Pacific. The bird pavilion was a metal-framed octagonal structure, which originally had open sides when it was located on the oceanfront boardwalk. The Commodore had originally constructed it as a dance pavilion prior to the construction of the casino. When the casino was completed, the pavilion was dismantled and transported up the hill to its present location, then renovated to include a building that served as a hospital for indigenous and migratory wildlife. As the museum's collection of artifacts grew, a portion of the pavilion was set aside for storage, cataloging, and restoration of recovered treasure.

Mrs. Rigney and I arrived outside the pavilion at the same time as Sir Arthur. Sumner Renton greeted us upon our arrival and invited us to follow him. The bird park was alive with the sounds of wild, exotic feathered creatures. I felt like I was in a Tarzan movie. There were no cages; instead, it was an immense open area under an octagonal canopy, enclosed by chain link fencing. There was tropical flora, trickling waterfalls, and a small brook. In the center of the open area were the animal hospital and artifacts vaults. Upon entering the vaults, one was struck with the ambiance of centuries-old treasure. The odor of barnacles, crustaceans, and bottom sediment was prevalent. Several volunteers were busy picking and scrubbing encrusted relics. Ships bells, coins, swords, helmets, and chest armor. It was a beehive of intense activity.

The good curator took us on an informative tour, showing the artifacts as they arrive from all points on the globe, then the step-by-step process of meticulous restoration and removal of organic build-up. Sumner, aware of our interest in the items from P.K.'s last expedition, saved those items for last.

Sir Arthur was positively beaming throughout the presentation and appeared to be enjoying himself immensely. He was bursting with intuitive questions and informative comments. Most of the metal objects were still encrusted with sediment and corrosion. Those items were kept submerged in a seawater tank, because of the rapid deterioration that occurred when such items were exposed to the air.

Sir Arthur gazed with obvious delight into the tanks that held a variety of artifacts. Though they were mutated with crustacean, the basic forms and shapes were still recognizable as weapons, coins, and an interesting stack of bars or ingots. One could image them to be gold or silver.

Sir Arthur was fascinated. He explained that the bars could, in fact, be nothing more than ceramic bricks with which to build small Buddhist shrines either aboard during a long journey, or in the yet to be conquered territory. "Fascinating," he beamed.

Finally, Sumner Renton opened a door to a vault housing an array of ceramic pots, vessels, and gourds, all intricately carved in the design and style known to be from the Zin Yuen Dynasty. Try as he might, Sir Arthur could not mask his excitement.

The good curator explained that they had concentrated on the restoration of the ceramic artifacts first because they were in more pristine condition and easier to restore. The pottery was not affected by rust, oxidation, or other deleterious elements, as metal objects would be.

Sir Arthur commended the curator on the variety of well-preserved objects on hand. "Very proliferous. Very impressive. Very impressive, indeed," he repeated on several occasions. Sir Arthur was positively giddy. He couldn't restrain himself and asked about gold and silver art objects, religious deities or statuary, his particular field of obsession.

Sumner Renton simply smiled and scratched his head. "You know," he began. "Seems like everybody lately is asking me about those types of items. It's perplexing, because I'm not aware of anything like that in connection with this expedition, yet everybody seems to think they do indeed exist."

"Ahhh!" laughed Sir Arthur. "Yes, indeed, my friend, as you no doubt are aware, there are well documented accounts of such objects having been aboard the ill-fated fleet. Whether those objects were commandeered by pirates centuries ago, or still lie at the bottom of the ocean is subject to much speculation, my friend. Either way, I can, with a certain amount of confidence, assure you that such objects do indeed exist."

We concluded our visit and thanked Sumner Renton for his indulgence and graciousness. We bid goodbye to Sir Arthur, joined Roscoe, who had waited for us, and returned to town. On the ride to town, Lara invited me to join her for lunch, and we asked Roscoe to drop us at the Decanso Beach entrance. Roscoe drove north through town and eventually came to a stop near the beach. Lara and I got out and walked a short distance along the shore until we came to a small cave that extended through a sheer rock outcropping that cut across the beach and into the surf.

Once we had crossed the cave, we emerged onto a shimmering white beach that curved in a gentle arc around a pristine, azure bay. Set back just off the beach was a sprawling, Victorian hotel with vine covered verandas, beautiful open patios, and wide expanses of bright green lawns. The Decanso Beach Hotel was the upscale hideaway for secluded love trysts of the Hollywood elite and the residence of choice for the authentically rich who visited Catalina.

Lara and I walked down the beach and into the patio restaurant where we were shown to an umbrella table on the deck overlooking the bay. Lara explained, over drinks, that Decanso Bay Beach was the site of the Mardi Gras celebration marking the end of this year's, weeklong carnival on the island. It was traditionally a combination Bacchanal celebration and luau, combining a pig roast and bonfire with Caribbean rhythms and open bar. It was a gigantic beach party where everyone let their hair down and danced the night away in reckless abandon. From her description, I imagined an exotic island rite of fertility. An erotic, multi-partnered sexathon. Perhaps I was reading more into it than was warranted. Maybe I was just very optimistic.

When we finished our crab salad and champagne brunch, Lara and I walked back along the beach toward the casino. As we strolled in the warm sun, I discussed my feeling about what could have compelled someone, or group of someones, to feel so threatened by Johnny's knowledge, that they would remove him permanently. My gut feeling was that it had to do with the casino or the Kubla Khan treasure. Or perhaps both.

I inquired as to any outside pressure that she was aware of regarding the operation of the casino. Was anyone trying to force his way into the operation? Was she aware of any skimming taking place, or extortion of any kind? Any threats or subversive manipulation? Any attempt to disrupt material or labor supply? Any arm's length maneuvering?

She pondered my questions quietly, and after some contemplation, her response was a hesitant negative. She was not aware of any specific threats or manipulation. She said, however, that Johnny was distant and preoccupied in the weeks before his disappearance. He seemed disconcerted, but never told her what was bothering him. She further stated that this behavior was not necessarily unusual for Johnny. He normally was introverted when concentrating on a problem, and rarely communicated his thoughts until he had formulated a decision.

"Most of Johnny's decisions," she added, "were thoroughly explored, examined from every angle, dissected, and inspected. Johnny always investigated every option available. It was like a game of chess with him. He knew all the angles, anticipated every move, and calculated the odds on all consequences before he articulated his position."

All but one, I thought to myself.

"This," she continued, "was in direct contrast to the process by which P.K. made decisions. He was impulsive, extroverted, and brash. It got him into trouble more often than not and fed the perception of him as untrustworthy, unreliable, and irresponsible. Johnny was considered levelheaded, conservative, and P.K. was characterized as a wayward Bohemian adventurer, unfettered by morals, scruples, or normal behavior. Hard to believe they both emerged from the same gene-pool."

She reminded me, however, that it was Johnny who had originally initiated the casino audit. He may have had suspicions regarding misappropriation or embezzlement.

When we reached the casino, we left the beach and continued our stroll south along the boardwalk. The sun was shining, the birds were singing, and the harbor area was alive with enormous billowing sails colorfully hoisted above the glistening decks of the many sleek yachts.

As we continued south along the boardwalk through town, I hesitantly handed the photograph I had received from Chin Lee to Lara. I asked her about the identities of the people in the picture, as I had Rita and Captain Wally. I wasn't sure anything she added would be worth the emotions, good or bad, that could be dredged from the memories.

Lara recognized the people in the foreground as Hollywood movie people, though she could not recall names or professions specifically. She stopped and stared at the picture quietly for some time. Finally, I asked her about the man in the background, previously identified as Nick Licatta. She said she may have met him sometime in the past, but couldn't remember who he was or what he did. She thought he was a relative of Nicky Fallon's, but she wasn't really sure.

She became very quiet and wearily handed the picture back to me. I knew it was nearing a sensitive subject, but I had to inquire. Lara told the same story about Johnny and Chin Lee that Captain Wally had. She had been aware of the close relationship Johnny and Chin Lee had when they were young, and the wrenching heartbreak both experienced later. She didn't have much to add, except that Johnny didn't talk about it much. She felt that he had come to terms with the realities of life and had reluctantly moved on. Chin Lee, however, still dealt with inner torment and anguish. Lara liked Chin Lee, and like many others locals, felt sympathy for her and tried to help as much as she would accept. Chin Lee seemed soft and vulnerable, but she had learned to take care of herself, and she was fiercely stubborn and independent.

Chapter 16

The Rendezvous

That evening, I chaperoned Mrs. Rigney to the closing event of the year's film fest. Tonight, a Buzby Berkley romantic musical comedy extravaganza. Once the film began, I excused myself and went in search of Chin Lee.

I arrived at the Blue Parrot early in the evening and found the establishment void of patrons. The bartender, having no intoxicants to concoct, was busy scribbling on a note pad behind the bar.

"Good evening, Mr. Dugan," he said. "What can I get for you?"

That's one of the alluring aspects of Avalon; it's a place to get away where everybody knows your name.

"How about something fruity, with little umbrellas in it," I said.

That, as it turned out, involved a tall, frosted glass, filled two-thirds with a pale blue liquid, a dollop of assorted fruit, an umbrella as requested, and a long stick, curved at the end that doubled as a back scratcher. Thus, the "Island Itch."

"What are you working on back there?" I asked.

He told me he was a bartender by night and an aspiring screenwriter by day. He was working on a story about a guy wrongfully convicted of murdering his wife. He escapes while en route to the penitentiary and electric chair. He then embarks on a search for a one-armed man he believes to be the real killer—all the while being pursued by a relentless federal marshal. That's another thing Avalon had in common with L.A.—everybody you meet is an actor, director, or screenwriter with a project in development. I wished him luck and advised him to keep his night job.

I asked if Chin Lee was scheduled to work tonight. He said that she was, but he had not heard from her, and she was late, which was unusual for her, as she was very conscientious and always on time.

The sun had set behind the mountain overlooking Avalon by the time I had finished my turquoise concoction. I paid my tab and left a hefty contribution toward the future Hollywood blockbuster. I exited the Blue Parrot in the subtle grey light of dusk. Destination, Chin Lee's.

As I made my way along the boardwalk, I became aware that I had acquired a tail. He hung back at a comfortable distance, attempting to blend with the other window shoppers, but there was little doubt that I was the object of his attention. He was a small, well-dressed Chinaman who followed discreetly at every course change. I made a few diversions from a steadfast heading, and he followed skillfully. I then turned a corner, ducked into a darkened alcove, and waited. He quickened his pace when I disappeared from view. As he passed, I put my .38 to the side of his head. "Freeze, Chinaman."

He obeyed my command, surprised. Then, in the blink of an eye, he simply reached across and firmly grasped the top of the revolver, pinning my hand with his, preventing the cylinder from rotating or the hammer from striking. In the next moment, he stepped behind me, twisting my arm behind my back, took the gun, and bent my hand forward until my fingers were touching the inside of my wrist. With minimum pressure to the back of my hand, he held me paralyzed in excruciating pain. I have to re-think this .38 revolver as an urban weapon concept.

"Okay, walk, round-eye," he said, and with the slightest pressure, we were headed up the street at a brisk pace. Within minutes, we were standing in the rubble of what once was Chin Lee's apartment. Several Chinese thugs were meticulously shredding every square inch of the apartment's interior. Chin Lee sat tied to a chair. She was gagged and hung limply from her restraints. She had been severely beaten and was barely conscious.

At that moment, the smarmy Tong Ahn Hai emerged from the bedroom. He looked at me, uttered some terse commands in Chinese, then walked over and punched me in the chest, knocking the wind out of me. I collapsed on the floor, gasping for air. After another hurried command, I was hog-tied, gagged, and thrown to the floor on my face. From my limited vantage on the floor, I counted four Tongs and Ahn Hai, who continued to rip apart the interior of Chin Lee's flat, searching for something.

Finally, apparently frustrated, Ahn Hai ordered his men out. A big black sedan pulled up out front, and Chin Lee and I were rudely dragged from the apartment and tossed into the back seat. The sedan sped through the darkened streets of Avalon, destination unknown.

After a long ride over open terrain, the sedan slowed and crossed the narrow causeway into Cooley Town. The car stopped in front of one of the many indistinguishable cabins in the Chinese camp, and we were hauled out, dragged inside, and tied to rickety chairs. The pungent aroma of kim chee was in the air—bringing with it a recollection of the days I spent in the Pacific during the war. A deep sense of foreboding swept over me. We were indeed in deep kim chee.

The interior of the cabin had been split into two rooms by a thin partition. Chin Lee and I were in a barren room with no furniture but a small wooden table and the chairs to which we were restrained. I looked at Chin Lee. She was conscious, but just barely. She was in a state of shock. Her eyes were open, but vacant, and she stared blankly at the floor. She was in bad shape. She had been worked over pretty thoroughly, but she apparently had not told them whatever it was they wanted to know.

Just then, I heard another car pull to a stop out front. There was a muffled conversation from within the adjoining room.

Then the door burst open and in walked Mr. Chang and Ahn Hai, followed by none other than Harold Peters, that slime-ball little puke. Peters smiled and walked over to where I sat tied to the chair. He removed the gag and bent close to my face.

"So, Mr. Dugan," he gloated in an irritating, condescending voice. "It appears as though you have—oh, what is that charming phrase that malcontents of your ilk use—stepped on your dick!"

Mr. Chang then said, "There is an ancient Chinese proverb, which loosely translated states, "There is nothing quite like that special feeling one gets when one realizes that he has screwed himself because he tried too hard to please everybody else."

"Blow it out your samurai-suckin' ass, fat boy," was my less than brilliant response. But to my personal satisfaction, it pissed him off. He backhanded me across the kisser then gave me a few more. Peters then stepped up and got in a few licks of his own. He grabbed me by the front of my shirt then brought his walleyed face close to mine.

"I told you I would repay you for slapping me around, re-member, Mr. Dugan?" he asked. "And throttling me with my collar," he said as he yanked back and forth on my shirt.

He worked himself into a froth until he pulled so hard that he tore open the front of my shirt, exposing the dog whistle that hung around my neck.

"What the hell is this?" he asked, taking the whistle in his hand.

"It's a boatswain's pipe," I responded. "A souvenir from the war. It doesn't work anymore. It's broken."

Harold Peters stared at the whistle. It was obvious that he had never seen a dog whistle or a boatswain's pipe. He held it in his hand for a moment, studying it, then stuck it in my mouth and said, "Blow."

I blew into it as he commanded. Of course, there was no au-dible sound emitted, and I shrugged my shoulders, as if to say, "Told ya so."

Suddenly a look of revelation spread across his face. He turned quickly toward Chin Lee. "Search her," he yelled. "Strip her clothes off and search every part of her body."

Ahn Hai immediately pounced on her and ripped her blouse and skirt off her. There, suspended by a delicate gold chain around her waist, hung a small silver key. There was a stunning silence. For a brief moment, time stood still.

Finally, Mr. Chang ripped the chain and key from her waist. "Kill them," he commanded.

I tried to leap to my feet, still restrained in the chair. I managed to get into a standing position as Harold Peters raised a small-caliber pistol and pulled the trigger. There was an explosive flash of light then everything faded to black. When I came to, I was lying face down in a warm, sticky pool of my own blood. I felt fuzzy. My ears were ringing, and there were spots before my eyes. I struggled to free myself from the pile of kindling that once had been the chair to which I was tied. I got to my feet and removed the restraints. I was groggy. I gazed over where Chin Lee had sat, straining to focus. She was lying on the floor, still tied to her chair, facing the wall. I hesitantly staggered to where she lay, afraid of what I might find.

She was lifeless on the floor, her throat slashed. Her blood flowed out onto the floor around her. I knelt beside her and cried. She was a sweet, innocent girl who had been dealt a tough hand. She had lived a rough life, through no fault of her own, and had courageously given that life trying to keep a secret a childhood love had entrusted to her.

When I had finally regained my composure and wiped my eyes, I noticed that Chin Lee, with her dying breath, had left a final clue. She had freed one of her arms, and with a finger dipped in her own blood, written on the inside of her thigh two words: dive locker.

"Dive locker?" I didn't know what that meant. I began to panic. "What the hell is a dive locker?" I said aloud. "I don't know what she's trying to tell me."

I got to my feet, picked my hat up off the floor, and staggered through the doorway into the adjoining room. I felt dizzy and looked down at my hat. My fingers protruded through a long, ragged tear in the side, just at the band. I felt alongside my head, above my right ear. A soft, mushy furrow was ripped through my scalp from front to back. The bullet had grazed the side of my head, but not penetrated the skull. I was a very lucky boy.

Outside, there was an apprehensive crowd of Chinese men and women gathered in the darkness. They stared at me in silence as I emerged from the cabin. The crowd parted as someone with authority approached. There, in the darkness, a small, spindly, elderly gentleman bowed humbly before me. "The Tong went that way by car, back toward town," he said, pointing south over the causeway.

"Is there another car here?" I asked.

"No car," he said. "You take boat. Fastest on island."

He hustled me down to a sleek-looking mahogany Chris Craft tied to a small pier. This boat, I thought, was very similar to the one owned by the Commodore. That is, until I turned the key in the ignition and fired her up. She roared to life—a fire-breathing, flying dragon.

"Do you know what a dive locker is?" I shouted to the old man as he untied the lines securing the boat to the pier.

"Dive locker?" he repeated. "Storage compartment on diver's pier in town," he said. "Dive locker—you go, take boat."

I pushed forward on the throttle and the boat blasted out of the water like a rocket. I redlined the RPMs and the engine screamed to life in a fine-tuned, high-pitched whine that propelled me, like a divine wind, through the dark night toward Avalon.

Chapter 17

The Race

Sir Arthur and his mutant Cro-Magnon finished picking over the remains of Chin Lee's possessions like a couple of bloated vultures, before they stepped onto the sidewalk out front. Suddenly, at the end of the street, the two black sedans carrying Mr. Chang and his band of thieves raced past in the mist, heading for town. Phangs Pa got behind the wheel of the car, Sir Arthur crammed his girth in next to him, and they sped off in pursuit.

Chang's sedan raced through town and pulled to a stop at the entrance to the divers' pier. The second sedan made an abrupt turn and headed up the hill toward the bird pavilion and the airport at the top of the mountain.

Chang, Peters, and Ahn Hai hurried down the pier that was laden with fishing nets, lobster traps, buoys, fenders, and all manner of diving equipment. They finally came to a section toward the end that was lined on both sides with stacks of storage compartments—dive lockers. They spread out on both sides and began searching for the locker with the number on it that matched the one on the key they had taken from Chin Lee. Two of the three Tongs waiting in the car at the end of the pier stepped out and scanned the boardwalk, guarding against unwanted intruders. In the light fog, the town appeared deserted.

With hushed excitement, Chang and the other two thieves quietly converged on the locker for which they had been searching. The two Tongs keeping watch on the entrance to the pier headed toward the locker as well.

Chang slipped the key into the lock. He turned the handle, and the door slowly opened. Harold Peters anxiously reached inside and withdrew a square wooden box the size of a small steamer trunk. He carried it over and set it on a stack of wooden crates. Carefully, they pried the box open. There, lying inside, was the intricate statue of a golden dragon encrusted with rubies and emeralds. A silence fell over the band of thieves; they had found Khan's golden dragon.

"Thank you, gentlemen," said Sir Arthur behind them, holding a small-caliber pistol. "If you will be so kind as to step away from the box so that I may take possession, I would be ever so grateful."

At this moment, I came around Casino Point and roared toward the divers' pier. I blew my dog whistle with all my might, hoping the inaudible sound would carry up the hill to the mansion. My thundering approach was all the distraction Mr. Chang needed. He swung his cane and brought it down across Sir Arthur's wrist, knocking the gun to the pier. A mad scramble ensued. Mr. Chang removed the headpiece of his cane and drew a razor-sharp sword. He attacked Sir Arthur, who fended off the blows with some skilled cane techniques of his own.

As I slammed the boat into the pier, Phangs Pa stepped out from behind a stack of crates and grabbed one of the hapless Tongs by his neck and his crotch. Phangs Pa lifted the man high overhead, and sent him head long through the canopy of the glass bottom boat tied to the pier. My .38 fell from the Tong's pocket and clattered to the ground as he crashed through the thick viewing glass at the bottom of the boat and plunged into the water. Ahn Hai then engaged Phangs Pa in mortal combat.

I climbed from the boat and was confronted by another Tong wearing a wide grin and brandishing a pointed dagger. I grabbed both of his feet and swept him to the pier with a thud. In the next instant, I was on top of him, holding down the knife with one hand and laying some solid punches with my other like a jackhammer. We rolled across the pier, crashing into a stack of lobster traps and bringing the entire stack down on everyone. When I finally freed myself from the tangle of traps and fishing nets, I found myself staring down the barrel of my own .38. Suddenly, from behind the Tong holding the gun came the menacing growl of one mean "some-bitch" by the name of Bogie. The smirk quickly faded as the Tong turned to face a snarling mouthful of fangs. Like a bolt of lightning, Bogie leaped from atop the crates and tore at his throat. He brought him down, viciously thrashing back and forth like a frenzied shark, ripping the man's throat clear to the spine.

Ahn Hai climbed from beneath the tangle of traps and nets just in time to become Bogie's next victim. The big black dog ran headlong at Ahn Hai, who put his arms up in front of his neck to ward off the attack. This time, however, Bogie latched onto Ahn Hai's groin, dragged him screaming along the pier, and mauled him to an agonizing death.

At that moment, the pier lit up with automatic gunfire. The Tong waiting at the entrance to the pier in the sedan began firing sporadic bursts down the pier, sending everyone diving for cover. Hot tracers zinged off the pier planks and traps and popped into the metal lockers and crates around us. Amidst the confusion, Peters grabbed the box containing the Golden Dragon and ran back down the pier toward the waiting car with Mr. Chang following close behind. They reached the sedan and leaped in as the Tong ceased fire and climbed behind the wheel. The sedan sped through town and up the mountain toward the airport. Phangs Pa and Sir Arthur hurried to their car and were in hot pursuit.

I scrambled from my hiding place and retrieved my .38 from the unfortunate Tong that Bogie had all but decapitated. I jumped back into my boat and blasted across the water in the darkness, past the shipping terminal and the seaplane tarmac. I had no idea where I was going, but the alternative was to stand on the pier and do nothing. So off I went through the darkness, past the rock quarry and around Seal Cove to the windward side of the island.

LaFarge was en route to the pier with a contingent of Gendarmes when Chang and Peters roared up the road in the opposite direction, hastily pursued by Phangs Pa and Sir Arthur. LaFarge's squad car turned around and hurried after the careening sedans. I passed Seal Cove on my starboard, the sleek Chris screaming flat out. The sun had begun to rise behind me, and I was able to navigate in the twilight of dawn.

A furious running gun battle ensued between Chang and Peters and the pursuing Sir Arthur and Phangs Pa. Up the narrow mountain road they sped. Round after round shattered windshields and punctured metal. Shrapnel flew like Fourth of July sparklers with each impact or ricochet. They careened onto the airport tarmac, tires screeching, and guns ablaze. A small twin-prop DC-3 sat warmed and ready at the end of the runway. The first rays of morning light blazed across the airport as Chang's sedan made a screeching stop behind the plane already beginning to roll. Chang, Peters, and the driver scrambled aboard as the tail dragger began its lumbering takeoff.

The plane began to gain speed as Phangs Pa and Sir Arthur roared onto the runway in pursuit. Entering the airport tarmac just behind was LaFarge and another patrol car that had joined the chase, lights and siren ablaze. The plane, now almost half-way down the runway, began to lift its tail wheel off the ground. It was within seconds of takeoff. Sir Arthur's sedan and La-Farge's police car raced down either side of the runway just behind the DC-3.

Machine-gun fire erupted from the open door of the plane, and LaFarge's car was hit in the right front tire, sending it barrel rolling down the concourse, disintegrating into pieces.

At the last second, Phangs Pa turned into the plane, crashing the sedan into the tail section, damaging the elevators and vertical stabilizer. The plane, now incapable of taking to the air, hurtled down the vanishing runway at breakneck speed.

The pilot, realizing the futility of takeoff, tried to slow the plane before it reached the end of the runway and plunged over the steep embankment into the rugged canyon below. He was not going to get her stopped in time. In desperation, he cut the port engine and gave the starboard full throttle. He smashed the left rudder to the floor. The plane began to skid across the runway, dragging the left wing tip and ripping off the tail wheel. He made a 180-degree ground loop, slammed the left throttle to the firewall, and headed back down the taxiway toward the airport entrance, dragging the damaged tail section in a flurry sparks.

The second patrol car stopped at the wreckage of LaFarge's car and the driver helped extricate the survivors of crash. Phangs Pa and Sir Arthur still pursued the runaway plane in the opposite direction from which they had come.

The plane careened down the runway until it finally crashed into one of the sedans left at the entrance. Peters, still clutching the Golden Dragon, Chang, and the remaining Tong leaped from the burning plane, ran for the other car, and raced away from the airport in the direction of Smuggler's Cove. Phangs Pa and Sir Arthur were right behind them, and the remaining police car soon hurtled down the narrow mountain road after them.

In Smuggler's Cove, a tanker truck hauling diesel fuel had just left the dock area after refueling Dr. Con's sleek motor yacht. As he approached the gates, leaving the compound, the three rampaging cars came down the road, virtually out of control. Having opened the gates to allow the tanker to exit, the guards ran for cover as the cars approached on a collision course with the fuel-laden truck.

The first two cars screamed past, barely avoiding the tanker. But the police car careened off the gateposts and slammed into the tanker, igniting a horrendous explosion that instantly vaporized the two vehicles and everyone inside. Flaming pieces of molten wreckage plunged off the road and down the steep cliff, scattering burning debris over the beach and into the water.

Peters and the Chinaman sped on through the compound and came to a screeching stop alongside Con's yacht. They emerged from the car and shot their way aboard. The Tong soldier raced to the engine room while Chang and Peters climbed the ladder to the bridge, seized the skipper, and commandeered the boat. They demanded, at gunpoint, that he put to sea immediately.

With a thunderous rumble of her diesels, the sleek yacht powered away from the dock and headed out of the cove in a desperate flight for open water. As I came around China Point, south of Smuggler's Cove, I spotted the yacht coming at high speed, a flotilla of Con's guards in pursuit. The guards, not knowing who was who, began firing at everything on the water, including me. They didn't realize I was trying to stop the boat, not run interference for it. I tried to outrun the yacht and get in front of it, but the barrage of gunfire coming from the guards' boats was chewing up the mahogany Chris and preventing me from getting too close.

I spotted Blaine Pond angling in on the yacht from the starboard side. He had been diving off the entrance to the cove. The yacht veered toward him and plowed through his boat amidships, slicing it in half. I struggled to keep pace with the fast moving yacht. The guards' boats were beginning to close in on us. They continued to fire, splintering my boat's hull.

Suddenly, out of nowhere, Captain Wally's tugboat appeared at a right angle to our course, full speed, and horn blasting. He cut across my wake and broadsided two of the guard boats, pulverizing them into splintered kindling, the nautical equivalent to the cavalry riding to the rescue.

Con's pirated yacht made a sudden course change, attempting to run over me. I tried several evasive maneuvers, but the powerful yacht was just too big and fast. It was closing on me quickly. I yanked the boat to port at the last second, but it was too late. The yacht plowed over the stern of my boat, tossing me into the water. It passed me so close that I had to push off with my feet as it swept by to keep from being run over. I was left adrift, treading water in the middle of a big, wide ocean.

Just then, coming in from the rising sun, Steve Canyon's small red sea plane made a low pass over my position then circled around and set down upon the surface of the water. He taxied over to where I floundered about, and I scrambled aboard. Once aboard, Canyon firewalled the throttles, gradually gaining speed as it bounced along the tops of the swells until she finally lifted off the surface and climbed laboriously skyward.

We made a low pass over Captain Wally's tug as he retrieved Blaine Pond from the shattered remains of his sinking boat. They gave us a thumbs-up and waved us toward the fleeing yacht as it ran for open water. As we chased the yacht out to sea, Steve Canyon turned to me and shouted, "Well Dugan, have you got any idea how we're going to stop that boat once we catch it?"

I felt like a dog that chases cars. What the hell do you do once you've caught it? I pulled out my .38. "All I have is my snubby," I said. "Make a pass over the bow; I'll put a few rounds into the bridge."

He just laughed.

I slid back the cockpit window on my side as we passed the port side of the yacht. The Tong on the flying bridge fired sporadic bursts from his automatic weapon, several rounds impacting on the fuselage of our plane.

We banked sharply over the bow of the yacht, and I put six shots through the forward windows of the wheelhouse. We made a tight circle and came around from behind for another quasi-strafing run. I quickly reloaded and put six more rounds into the bridge. It was futile. We were not going to stop that boat with a snub-nose .38. What I wouldn't have given for a fifty-caliber mounted in the nose of that bird. We took several more hits and the starboard engine began to sputter and trail a wisp of smoke.

"Well, Dudley, you got anymore do-right ideas?" he yelled. "Cause we're not going to be able to keep up with them on just one engine."

"What else have we got?" I shouted back.

He turned to me with a sly grin. "We could do a kamikaze," he hooted. "I've always wanted to try that."

Yikes, this crazy bastard was nuts-oidal. I looked at him quizzically. It didn't seem a viable option to me.

"No, really, I've worked it all out," he shouted. "We'll do a touch and go off the water and fly her right into the side of the boat. You'll love it. We'll bail on the first hop."

I wasn't convinced, but he seemed sure it was doable.

"Okay, affirmative," I howled. "If you think it's possible, let's do it."

"Piece of cake," he yelled.

Yeah, right. Just don't turn us into fudge brownies, fly-boy.

We circled around and came in low on the starboard side. He throttled back and brought her in low and slow.

"Get ready," he said. "Open the door, and when I yell now, we jump."

We came in closer, closer; finally, we touched down. He immediately pulled back on the yoke and the plane began to lift off again. "Now!" he yelled, and we dove out of the plane as she began to rise above the surface of the water. The plane struck the starboard side of the bridge with a horrific explosion.

I hit the water with a bone-shattering impact and bounced along the surface for several yards before slowly settling limply into the deep, blue water. It was a hard landing, but not as bad as the one Lara Rigney and I took when her roadster plunged over the cliff into Lover's Cove.

The plane's impact and explosion destroyed the bridge of the yacht, but she continued on course, full-speed ahead and out of control. She was a runaway. Once again, I found myself bobbing about in the big wide ocean like flotsam and jetsam. Steve Canyon swam over and we hauled ourselves onto floating debris.

From behind us in the distance came the loud blast of ship's horn. We turned and saw a steaming Coast Guard cutter coming fast. It pulled alongside, and a rope ladder was lowered over the starboard side. We scrambled up the ladder and climbed aboard.

A familiar voice from afar welcomed us aboard. I looked up. It was Inspector Lugar, LAPD. "Another fine mess you've gotten me into," he said.

"What brings you out here, inspector?" I asked, surprised to see him.

"We had a body wash up off Newport Beach the other day," he said. "The coroner has tentatively identified it as one Harold Peters, occupation—accountant, from Chicago. Once I got that report, I figured you probably stepped on your widget again. So, here I am."

As soon as we were aboard, the cutter raced out to intercept Con's runaway boat. The yacht was moving through the water at full-speed, superstructure ablaze, trailing a massive plume of dark smoke. Her present course would take her just off San Clemente Island to the south, then across some very busy shipping lanes. She had to be stopped.

Kamikaze-boy and I were called to the bridge of the cutter. When we arrived, the captain asked what the situation was with the runaway yacht and who was aboard. I filled him in as quickly as I could, as we raced across the water attempting to intercept her.

A report from the cutter's combat information center indicated that the runaway was going to miss San Clemente Island, but radar had picked up a large ship in its projected path. The report identified the ship as the petroleum tanker *Valpriso*, currently loaded to the gunnels with high-octane aviation fuel. A sudden sense of alarm swept over the captain and crew on the bridge.

"Sound battle stations, lieutenant," the captain barked. "Let's get that forward gun manned and operational. Helmsman, sound all ahead full. We have to get within range of that boat before she collides with the tanker. Radioman, alert the *Valpriso* of the situation and have the skipper initiate whatever evasive maneuvers he deems necessary!"

The captain peered intently through his binoculars and said aloud, "Jesus Christ, if that boat hits that petroleum tanker, we're gonna have one helluva conflagration out here." He popped the cap on the blowpipe and yelled into it. "Engine room, we need more speed. I need more power, if you please, Mr. Scott."

CIC began to continuously sound bearing and range of the target, which was moving away from our position at high speed. Aboard the *Valpriso*, the skipper had the runaway boat in sight.

"Shit!" he yelled. "Hard to starboard. Sound general quarters!"

The impact, at present course, would occur on the port bow of the fuel-laden tanker. A ship that size doesn't turn on a dime. It requires several miles of open ocean to complete a direction change.

The tanker captain's intent was to turn to the starboard, thereby moving the point of impact further to the stern, then go back hard to port, and swing the stern out of the way at the last moment, allowing the runaway to pass on the port side. Two harried maneuvers to get both vessels on a parallel port side pass. Nothing else had any hope of avoiding a catastrophic collision. The tanker wasn't capable of maneuvering quickly enough to do anything else.

Back aboard the cutter, CIC had plotted course and speed of the runaway and reported that we were not going to get within range before impact. The captain ordered the forward gun to commence firing anyway. Several volleys were fired, and as expected, they fell short of the target. The captain attempted to skip rounds off the surface of the water and score a hit to the rudder or prop, much the same as skipping a flat stone off a lake or pond.

Before the order was given to cease fire, they managed to score a hit with a skipped round, but it exploded into the already burning superstructure and did nothing to impede the progress of the runaway yacht.

The target was getting too close to the tanker to continue firing. The chance of bouncing a round into the tanker was too great. As the flaming runaway approached, the skipper of the tanker ordered "hard to port, full ahead." The helmsman began to furiously spin the ship's wheel to the left. It was too late; the tanker was not going to clear its stern before the yacht hit.

The runaway swept by the tanker's bow on the port side and continued down the length of ship until it finally struck the stern and exploded, rocking the crew and blowing out the windows of the wheelhouse. The impact also damaged the tanker's rudder, making it unresponsive to commands from the bridge. The tanker was now headed toward San Clemente Island, incapable of altering its course.

The captain pulled himself up from the deck, and after assessing the extent of the damage to his vessel, ordered, "Abandon ship!"

The tanker, now herself a runaway, careened through the sea on a course that would send her into the sheer cliffs along San Clemente's rugged northern coast. There was no time to lower lifeboats or send out an SOS. The crew scrambled up on deck, leaped over the side, and fell the two stories to the water below.

The fuel-laden petroleum tanker collided, full-speed, into the sheer granite face of San Clemente's rugged cliff with an explosion to rival an atomic bomb. The tremendous blast shattered windows throughout the city of Avalon some thirty miles away and produced a mushroom cloud visible from the mainland.

The tanker was blown to smithereens, and the surface of the ocean became a conflagration of fire and brimstone. Flaming debris and smoldering fragments rained down from the sky into the relentless sea leaving no trace of the ship. All that remained was the scorched cliffs.

It was over. The sea had reclaimed Kubla Khan's treasure, and consumed all those who had conspired to possess the ill-fated trove. All were vanquished, returned to the sea...

Epilogue

"Well, Precious, there you have it—the complete itinerary of my Santa Catalina Island vacation, such as it was. We didn't solve the missing person's case for which I was originally summoned. We didn't recover the Kubla Khan treasure, though the whereabouts of the bronze seal has never been established. And it is unlikely that the Golden Dragon will be recovered anytime soon, because the yacht and its ill-begotten treasure sank off San Clemente Island into Scripts Canyon, one of the deepest undersea chasms on earth. It occurs to me that the treasure may be cursed. Everyone that encounters the treasure of Kubla Khan meets an untimely death and is delivered to the bottom of the sea.

"We did manage to curtail the careers of several infamous bad boys, but still others have yet to be dealt with, such as Dr. Con and Nicky Fallon. This particular chapter has ended for now, but I'm sure we will be back because the entire story has not yet been uncovered.

"As it turns out, Mr. Chang was indeed working for the Chinese government, only it wasn't the Nationalists, as he had indicated, but the Communists, operating from the mountains in the northern part of the country, near Mongolia.

The unidentified myopic accountant masquerading as Harold Peters apparently bumped off the real Harry Peters during the channel crossing and assumed his identity. He was obviously operating in conjunction with Chang and his band of Tongs, but the how and why went to the bottom along with the Golden Dragon.

"By the way, Precious, according to Inspector Lugar, the phone number that I surreptitiously notated outside Nicky

Fallon's office was the number to "Gazzardi's" on the strip. The proprietor of the popular Italian restaurant is none other than Frances 'Fat Frankie' Fallentino, a local Dominick Licatta lieutenant and brother-in-law. Get it? Nicky Fallon, Frank Fallentino, Dominick Licatta. Nicky Fallon is in reality Dominick Licatta's nephew. I still feel that pressure on the casino, though unsubstantiated, and the disappearance of Johnny Rigney originated from this source. I'm not finished here. I'll be back.

"And then there's the Rigney family itself. As I said in the beginning, the general perception is that the Commodore and Johnny ruled their domain with an iron fist. They are regarded in the corporate world as savvy, ruthless, and cunning, but I found them completely contrary to popular belief. I believe the Commodore and the entire Rigney family are genuinely caring and concerned individuals, keenly aware of their special position within society and among their fellow men. They are staunchly patriotic and conduct themselves with paternalism toward the island of Santa Catalina and its colorful inhabitants.

"The island is a wondrous place, and the Rigney family has made concerted efforts to ensure that it will remain so for the enjoyment of generations to come. I, for one, feel a special attraction for this romantic and natural, unspoiled island paradise. In fact, I arranged to attend the carnival at Decanso Beach the closing night of the island festival. The experience fell somewhere between the raunchy beach party that Lara described and the pagan sexathon I had lecherously imagined. Lots of primal dancing and savage behavior around the bonfire. Drinking and debauchery. Inhibitions were dropped quicker than the transparent sarongs and flowered leis that the ladies wore. There were more clandestine rendezvous in the palm groves adjacent to the beach than in the pool cabanas at a Hollywood cocktail party. That evening, the hills were alive with sound of muse.

"And finally, Precious, there are the beautiful and alluring Rigney women. Lara—cool, statuesque, and smoldering with intense sexuality. A world-class lady with keen intelligence, sophistication, and stunning beauty. I am honored to be counted among her friends, and I respect and thoroughly enjoy her strength of character, depth of compassion, and her stiletto-like wit. As I stated before, she is indeed a thoroughbred.

And Rita—dark, sensuous, exuberant, and vivacious. I've never had more fun with a woman in my entire life. She's child-like and bubbly, yet exotically sensual and uninhibited. She exudes primitive eroticism, the likes of which I have never experienced before. Her searing passion boils the blood and fuels the flames of desire. You know, Precious, this could be the beginning of a beautiful friendship."

THE END

Until "THE BIG GUN"
Return to Avalon.

Writers Guild of America, west, Inc.
Intellectual Property Registry
7000 West Third Street
Los Angeles, California 90048-4329
Telephone: 323-782-4500
Fax: 323-782-4803

Documentation of Registration

The Writers Guild of American, west, Inc. issues
this certificate to:
Gregory G. Goodloe

for the material entitled:
THE BIG CASINO

by the following:
GREGORY G. GOODLOE – Writer

Registration#: 1119342
Material Type: BOOK   Effective Date: 03/17/06
Registered By: GREGORY G. GOODLOE   Expiration
Date: 03/17/11